Other Book...

HOLLY WILD: Bamboo...
HOLLY WILD: Let Sle...
Lissy-Lost!

WELCOME TO DA UPPER PENINSULA DONCHAKNOW!

Thank you times ten to my GeEK Team: Marie, Lisa, Matt, Lynn and Karin, and to those who made this exploration possible, the Friends of the Porkies

This book is totally Michigan-made and printed on 100% recycled paper!

Library of Congress Cataloging-in-Publication Data

Taylor, Lori

Holly Wild (Book 3) : Packing For the Porkies—1st U.S. Edition

First Printing, Sept. 2013

Summary: Ten-year-old explorer, Holly Wild, travels with her Team to the Upper Peninsula home of her Wild relatives and Michigan's largest state park, the Porcupine Mountains Wilderness. Holly learns about teamwork and survival in the Wilderness in order to survive family foes, foibles and an encounter with forest folk legend Bigfoot.

ISBN 978-0-615-87321-3

[1. Nature—fiction. 2. Upper Peninsula—fiction. 3. Wilderness—fiction. 4. Science—fiction. 5. Forest—fiction.]

Library of Congress Control Number: 2013915395

Published in the U.S.A., September 2013

by Bear Track Press, Pinckney, MI

Printed in the U.S.A. by Edward Bros. Malloy Inc., Ann Arbor, MI

www.loritaylorart.com

HOLLY WILD: Packing for the PORKIES!

by

Lori Taylor

Bear Track Press
Pinckney, MI

PORCUPINE MOUNTAINS WILDERNESS STATE PARK

Lake Superior

SUMMIT PEAK

M-64

1. UNION BAY CAMPGROUND
2. SUMMIT PEAK
3. LAKE OF THE CLOUDS
4. ARTIST CABIN
5. PRESQUE ISLE RIVER
6. MANABEZHO FALLS
7. BIG CARP RIVER TRAIL (ESCARPMENT)
8. NONESUCH

What is this place, this wilderness?
Who are these Wild people? How do they live?
I shall have to befriend them. Get to know them. Win their trust.
Shall I trade with them for information and goods? Establish
communication and friendship? Do these wild folk of Michigan's
Upper Peninsula know of such things as mega malls,
the internet or cell phones? From family photos I've seen they
have the look of a wandering wolf at midnight, a porcupine
in a poplar pondering the dusk, a lone loon wailing on
a lake in a thrashing storm. Who are these forgotten
clans of a forgotten tribe?
They are—the Yoopers.

Holly H. Wild

Team Wild GeEKS

Day 1 (Sunday)

Destination: Porcupine Mountains Wilderness State Park

Her cries of pain pierced the still morning air, cries seldom heard by modern day human ears, cries like that of a birthing moose or a dying elk.

"No!" pleaded Gram as she fondly patted Bessie's rust-colored sides. "Not now, old girl, come on!" Bessie heaved and wheezed.

"Lord a'mighty, Kitty, she's on her last legs." Gram was sweating in the August heat.

"At least we aren't out in the middle of nowhere yet. See if you can get her down this next road," encouraged Aunt Kitty. She wore a look of growing concern and Hunter, her drool machine basset hound, whined softly, understanding the gravity of the situation.

"It's serious," I whispered to my Team. They looked at me. I shook my head slowly. It didn't look good.

My Team, twins Tierra and Sierra Hills, are my best friends and GeEKS (Geo-Explorer Kids). Tierra, or "T", is the artist/secretary while her twin Sierra, or "Sie", is our vice-president/researcher/photographer. And I, Holly H. Wild, am the president of the GeEKs and all around explorer. I am the one who gets dirty. I am the one who reports my gross and unusual nature clue finds to the Team and they research and record it. I am the one who usually gets myself into weird trouble times ten. And they are usually the ones who get me out.

"How much longer does she have, Gram?" I shut my eyes. I did not want to think about this unexpected turn of events. Aunt Kitty was on her phone speaking in hushed tones. We were so close to the U.P. and yet so far.

Since leaving Sleeping Bear Dunes National Lakeshore this morning, we had endured countless Hunter breaks and educational lectures from my nature-crazy Aunt Kitty. We passed cornfields, orchards, and giant windmills scraping the sky. And here we were, mere minutes from the Mackinac Bridge and trouble was already upon us!

Aunt Kitty pointed for Gram to turn onto Trails End Road. How fitting a name.

"Gang, our Porcupine Mountain Wilderness State Park adventure is taking a slight detour," Gram yelled to us in the back seat. Hunter found a suitcase handle to snack on in the rear of the van.

We turned down the fateful road and drove past a sign that read "Wilderness State Park", where a family posed for photos. I sighed with relief—wilderness. For a moment, I thought we'd be stuck in some noisy hotel in Mackinaw City, jam-packed with tourists and sightseers.

"Come on girl," Gram coaxed. "Just a little further. Then you can rest." Bessie quivered and quaked, saying her goodbyes. She made a soft sputtering sound and finished with a deep hacking cough, the kind that usually hits Gram early in the morning. Then she was silent.

"Well, we made it—almost," said Aunt Kitty. She snapped her phone shut, unbuckled, and jumped out to go find a park ranger.

"Glad this didn't happen on the bridge," said Gram. We all got out and looked at Bessie. The 15-year-old rusted out mom-van was more than a friend—she was family. But she had officially expired, ceased to be.

Gram gave a whistle as she inspected Bessie's underbelly. "Her carriage bolts rusted clean through. She coulda dropped her engine on the highway in who-knows-where," Gram said. "You got us here safely, Bess. You done good—real good."

"But wait—now what, Gram?" I asked. "What about the U.P., our vacation, Aunt Kitty's meeting?"

"Don't you worry, Holly," winked Gram. "It's all under control. Help will be here soon."

Our ultimate destination is the Porcupine Mountains Wilderness State Park. Our purpose is two-fold: Aunt Kitty was called to a meeting, and weird luck has it that my Team's mother, Misty Hills, is there for her artist-in-residence stay.

Finally, a State Park ranger in a forest-green uniform zipped up in his forest-green golf cart and loaded up our gear. The van had not made it as far as a campsite. Gram spoke with him briefly then waved for the Team and I to start walking and follow them through the towering pine trees.

"We'll have to be brave and rough it," I said to the Team, "out here in the Wilderness, waiting for a ride to the Upper Peninsula."

To me, the U.P. has always been that magical land of moose and wolf, where lumberjacks and miners dance with bears and sing into the night. It was the home of my Wild kinfolk and the birthplace of my Wild cousin (once removed) Pauline Bunyan.

During one of Aunt Kitty's lectures I had found a chewed up copy of a book under my seat that talked about the early explorers of Michigan. The book was really thick so I skipped over the parts with lots of words and went to the cool parts that mentioned birch-bark canoes, furs, beaver pelts and Indians.

With my Wild camping experience back at Sleeping Bear Dunes being cut short, I had been looking forward to a real rough and rugged adventure. Now I was overcome with excitement to explore the unknown, untamed U.P. and camp under the stars in the wilderness.

Most explorers had some kind of delay in their journey, so I was trying to take ours in stride and fought off stomach-grabbing panic. I did not want to have our trip of a lifetime into the wild reaches of Michigan canceled.

T and Sie knew all about my relatives who explored the New World. Great, great, great Aunt Daisy Crocket Wild, who wrassled a bear and saved her famous brother, and Aunt Jenny Appleseed, who wandered the Ohio Valley. But it was my Wild cousin Pauline Bunyan, our very own "Yooper", (a name for someone raised in the U.P. of Michigan), who I was curious about now.

Cousin Pauline

Like Pauline, I wanted to venture into the unknown and explore its rocky depths, to wander the forested places where my Wild relatives had trod. I had already wrassled a caiman on Beaver Island and danced with bear cubs in Sleeping Bear Dunes. What great mysterious adventure awaited me in the Porkies?

One of the other beasts I've faced is Ivy Buckthorn. Ivy is the biggest, loudest, meanest spoiled brat at Hayfields Elementary and is Team Wild's Arch-Enemy Number One. She had nearly spoiled our adventures on Beaver Island and at the Dunes. With her father in the hospital and her mom being pregnant, I was confident that we would not see her again until school started.

Aunt Kitty had told us that a wilderness area was an undeveloped and protected zone used by wild species, "a place that has not been significantly modified by human activity." The most intact, undisturbed wild natural areas left on our planet.

But we rounded the corner into the campground and it was all I could do to keep from freaking out. A flock of RVs gleamed in the afternoon sun, complete with satellite dishes, screen rooms and outdoor carpeting. Campers bustled from beach to bathhouse, and others ate lunches or took naps in the shade of neighboring RVs. The smells of pine, diesel and burnt toast filled the air along with the screeching of gulls and babies and yapping dogs and adults.

"*This* park is named Wilderness?" I demanded. My freckles crackled and popped as I watched a woman taking her cat for a walk in a covered stroller.

"I guess if you compare this to Mackinaw City, it *seems* like wilderness," Sie commented, one eyebrow raised.

Gulls wheeled closer looking for treats. I had learned my lesson earlier in the summer on feeding gulls. Just don't! One mottled gull flew low overhead screaming *"keeya-keeyaw"*, like it was warning us.

I turned around in time to pull T out of the path of a couple of kids racing on bikes. They just missed hitting her as they whizzed past. "Creeps," Sie mumbled.

The blonde, short-haired girl looked back with icy blues eyes and wicked grin.

"Sorry!" the boy with the bobbing dreadlocks called over his shoulder to us.

We wandered open-mouthed through the campground. "Polar bear Christmas lights," T whispered, "do *not* go with western fiesta lanterns. Tacky."

"Intense," said Sie, snapping shots of stacked kayaks, paper lanterns and neon tents. "Get it? In tents! Hah!" T and I groaned. "This wilderness park doesn't seem very wild to me. But it is interesting."

More kids zipped past on scooters and bikes, some no older than the twins' two-year-old sister, Savannah. RVs toted boats, tubes, and canoes. Trucks, trailers and pop-up campers sported flags, while towels, shorts and socks waved from clotheslines. A few tiny tents were sprinkled here and there. We watched a pack of bold, winged-scavengers raid an untended camp kitchen.

We found our pile of gear in the site next to a monstrous

RV. High-tech and huge, it was black and chrome and looked like the Death Star from *Star Wars* with its expando rooms, satellite dishes and air conditioning units jutting out in all directions.

"I can almost see Darth Vader stepping out of that thing," said Sie. "Cloak swirling and all."

"Hey, there's a Wookiee," I joked. A large, hairy, barefooted guy in floral shorts was sitting on a cooler playing video games next to the Death Star, while four wieners roasted on a stick.

"Whoever it is, they must have a bunch of Stormtroopers," said T, pointing at the army of brand new hybrid bikes leaning against the side.

"All the RVs have majestic, far-seeing eagles and muscle-ripped cougars painted on them in rugged outdoor settings," I said. "What a joke. This isn't real camping, it's cheating. Real camping is done in a tent."

Just then we heard a roar and rumble like an ore ship pulling into harbor, scraping boulders and rocks and gearing down its engines. Tree branches ripped and swayed. It reminded me of the scene in Jurassic park where the T-rex exploded through the forest. An ancient, duct-taped, yellowed RV pushed through the pines, sending needles and cones flying and squirrels scattering.

"What the…" laughed Sie. "Some doofus is trying to park their RV—badly." The swaying vehicle backed into a cooler of iced beverages, then tore down a clothesline of swimsuits. A rainbow of swim tubes rolled every which way. The thing rocked and rolled like an old pirate ship and creaked when it finally came to rest.

Then the rusted door screamed open. We three stood with our mouths open.

"Dad?" I croaked.

"Mr. Wild?" Sie guffawed. T elbowed her.

The next hardship I was to endure? My dad.

WILDERNESS STATE PARK
—THAT IS NOT WILDERNESS!

Don't get me wrong. My dad's a super guy. He's smart and tries hard to be funny, but he is, well, an embarrassing nerd-klutz, times three.

"Hi honey," Dad said, waving at me. On his way to meet us he tripped over a swim tube and flew forward, his scruffy face coming in for a crash landing. But at the last second he caught himself on a nearby electrical post.

"Mr. Wild, are you okay?!" asked T, looking horrified.

"Sure, yep, good to go, Sierra," he answered, scruffling his rusty-red bedhead.

"I'm Tierra," T said, smiling.

"Wow, Wolff! That was some parking job," said Gram, hopping out the other door.

"Gram? How did you end up with Dad?" I asked.

"Well," she said, smiling. "Your Dad was going to meet us in the Porkies as a surprise. When Bessie was in her death throes we called him and had him come meet us here."

Aunt Kitty came around the corner of the RV with Hunter. Hunter immediately slobbered up Dad's khaki shorts.

"Ah, Hector, good to see you, too," Dad said weakly.

Hunter

"Change in plans girls," said Aunt Kitty, tittering her elfin giggle. The Team and I looked at each other then back at Aunt Kitty. I didn't like the sound of this. Already things had gone south as we tried to go north.

"Actually, change in your ride," said Gram. "You're getting new wheels to get you to the Porcupine Mountains." Gram swept her hand wide at Dad's new vehicle purchase like it was a game show grand prize.

"*That's* our ride?" T gulped.

"I am not crossing Lake Michigan in that beat up thing," whispered Sie.

"Holy creeps!" I yelped. "This is awesome!"

"Yep," Dad said, wiping dog goo off his shorts. "She's all ours, Sunshine, all 26 feet of her. Ain't she a beaut? Got a good deal on her, too."

"I'll bet you did," said Gram, examining the shiny bald tires and water dripping from its underbelly.

"All she needs is a little TLC. They don't make 'em like this anymore. She's an '89 class C rig," Dad beamed.

"An '89? As in 1889?" quipped Sie.

"But whoa, wait—back up a minute!" I said, looking Gram in the eye. "You said *you* and *you're*. Don't you mean *our*, and *we're*?"

"Well, Sugar Lumpkins," Gram started. Gram only calls me silly baby names when something horrific is about to go down. "You see, I have to stay with the van to take care of the old girl's remains," Gram said, looking away.

Gram's not going with us? Our van, not going with us?! The two have been around since as long as I can remember! They're family. Both had been there the day I was born waiting to take me home. Both had taken us kids to our first day of

Kindergarten, the library and when we went out to scour the streets for road-kill. The drive to Empire must have been too much for the old girl.

I'd miss Gram, too. She taught me how to climb trees, catch snakes and skin the road-kill we found. Gram gave me her old hand-me-down backpack that became my new old backpack, her old hat and her heirloom Wildcat tail from Daisy Crockett-Wild. I had a tight feeling in my stomach. She had taught me all she knew. Now, except for my Team, I was on my own.

"Entre vous," Dad said, opening the door and snapping me out of my own head. He pulled down the step and both of us tripped up into the cabin of the old creaking vehicle.

I looked around. My eyes immediately locked on the bunk bed over the cab. "I get dibs on the bunk," I called out. It was a cool, high lookout place and it had its own little curtain to seal me off when I am journal writing.

"Hey, there's a tiny bathroom!" said Sie, peeking in the door.

"The dining area doubles as a bed," Dad said proudly.

"There's a microwave and a fridge, awesome time ten!" I said. The fridge was full of a good supply of Dad's cooking specialty, eggs and peanut butter, and half-frozen water bottles.

"The fridge doesn't work so frozen pop bottles keep things cold." Dad said.

T moved to the rear of the rig. The back bedroom had a double bed with glow-in-the-dark

HOME SWEET ROLLING HOME

stars on the ceiling.

"The pink carpeting and rubber ducky in the bathroom don't really say 'wilderness'," said Sie.

"It's actually Dusty Rose, Sharon, not pink," said Dad, "the color of an evening desert sky."

"A sky back in the 80s maybe," mumbled Sie. "And it's Sierra, Mr. Wild." She poked her finger through a hole in the faded trout-patterned curtains.

"I think she's cool," I said, opening drawers and cabinets, looking for secret diaries or artifacts. "What's her name? The RV, I mean." Every vehicle in the Wild household had a name.

"The Beast," Dad beamed. She was a beast, too, like she had been through battles. The Beast must be Dad's "midlife crisis" car. You always hear about guys getting one when they get old, like when they're in their 30s. They want a new car to feel young again, although in dad's case this was almost as old as he was—more like a BFF or high school buddy.

"She's seaworthy and shipshape." Dad said, pushing up his glasses, then turned and smacked his head on the stove hood, knocking them off.

"Are we staying here, at this campground?" I asked, as Aunt Kitty began transferring our gear inside the hold.

"Nope. Gram is staying," Aunt Kitty replied. "Your mom is coming up to get her with my car. But we are leaving right now." I was glad to hear we weren't staying here in this "wilderness." I wanted real Porcupine Wilderness—wild woods and water.

"I'm ready to rumble," Dad said, gathering up maps that had tumbled onto his head from the visor. "Had a gallon of coffee already. And I'm hoping our little adventure will inspire me for new characters for a comic I'm working on. Oh, and to spend some time with you kids."

Gram brought in the last load of gear and dumped it on the

bed in back. Hunter climbed up with his short legs and made a nice nest next to the gear pile.

"Well, don't get all sentimental," she said. "You kids have a long road ahead. Better hit it." Gram gave us all squeezes then shook my hand.

"From one explorer to another. This is your big moment Holly." She blinked a few times then said, "Listen to the trees. Trees are in our Wild blood." With that, she climbed down the RV steps and closed the door. My stomach felt creepy.

"Supplies loaded. Fully stocked," Dad grinned. "We're ready to hit the road!"

The Beast chugged and lurched and with a crunching thud we were off, dragging along a lawn chair. The Beast eats everything in its path. Gram waved and I waved back. She looked so tiny standing there alone. I blinked back tears.

I still couldn't understand why Dad of all people was going camping, even if it was in an old RV. He hates the outdoors. He was the only Wild that did. Must be that midlife crisis thing.

Chapter 3

INTO THE WILD YOOPERLAND

Aunt Kitty was in the galley fixing sandwiches for lunch. T's stomach growled on cue. The twins started playing cards at the table. I sighed and joined the Team, sliding in next to Sie at the dining table. I tried to get my mind off Gram by writing in my journal. I imagined myself writing my entries by candlelight.

> Quarters are tight. Sie sniffles. There is a presence of disease, but she assures me it's just allergies. I'm not taking chances. It is my destiny to study these people, the tribe of Yoopers. It is my quest to camp in the Wilderness beneath wild stars. The failed attempt at Sleeping Bear Dunes brought me much disappointment.

"Holly, you're such a dork," said Sie.

"Hey, don't look over my shoulder!" I cried, throwing my body across my journal.

We stopped for gas in Mackinaw City. I was excited because the sign read "Gas, Souvenirs and Nightcrawlers."

"Dad," I said sweetly, "Can I get a souvenir? You know,

something to remember our time together by." Gram had given me some money, but it never hurts to ask.

"Um, sure Sunshine," he said, his head under the Beast's hood, checking her oil. "Here's a twenty. Bring me the change. Oh, and get a couple of bags of ice. The bottles in the fridge are almost melted."

"Sure!" I snatched the bill from his hand and ran inside. Aisles of touristy goodness awaited me. The twins were doing their value shopping, reading labels and counting change. I knew exactly what I wanted. Thirty dollars and forty five cents later I was back in the RV with one bag of ice and my bulging bag of wonders. The Beast roared to life once again.

"Didja get the ice?" Dad asked as he wheeled onto the road, taking out a decorative deer statue in the process.

"Sure did," I beamed, clutching my bag to my chest. "I even put it in on top of the food in the fridge."

"Super," Dad shouted over the mighty engine rumble. "You got change for me? I have to pay the bridge toll soon."

"The bridge troll?" I shouted. "What's that?"

"*Toll*, not troll Holly," Aunt Kitty said, setting our lunch down. "Although people who live in the U.P. sometimes call those of us who live in the Lower Peninsula trolls because they live 'under' the bridge. We have to pay to get across."

I withered. Oops. "Um, I don't have it on me now." Sie looked over her glasses at me. I slid down into my seat.

But Aunt Kitty just winked at me and dug some bills out from her vest pocket. I cringed and nibbled my crust silently.

"So what did you buy, Holly?" T asked, eyeing the bag.

"Stuff to use in the woods. Stuff I need." I shrugged. I felt like I was in the hot seat, but that might have been from the engine throwing heat off like a furnace. T showed me her three flavors of fudge, and Sie pulled out a t-shirt that read "Say Ya to Da U.P., eh."

"Now you," Sie said, squinting at me. I fished around inside the bag.

"Um, this." I pulled out a pen with canoes that floated inside. Sie and T eyed my still-bulging bag. I slid it behind me.

"Cards anyone?" I asked, grinning and holding up the deck. I wanted to reveal my surprise when the time was right.

"Hang on kids, here we go!" Dad cried over the roar of the Beast. "We're about to cross the Mighty Mac!"

The Mackinac Bridge loomed ahead. Tall and ominous, the steel and concrete suspension structure gleamed in the sun. T closed her eyes. Sie stared straight ahead. I pressed my face up against the window and looked over the edge.

"If we tip over into the lake we might see sturgeon and stuff," I said, combing the water for ancient fish.

Just then a huge black and chrome RV honked and whizzed past us.

"Hey, safety first, mister!" my dad called to the driver. But they were long gone.

"That looked like that Death Star," I said to Sierra.

"I don't even want to know," she said, staring intently at a crumb on the table. "Just tell me when we get to the other side."

The Beast chugged ahead like an ore boat crossing the churning waters below. Tiny boats zipped across the deep blue lake spraying water in their wake.

"Lake Michigan is on the left and Lake Huron on the right," hollered Aunt Kitty from the passenger seat. "They're separated by the Straits of Mackinac. That's Mackinac Island over there, home of fudge, fort and the Governor's mansion. You can see the Grand Hotel there," she pointed.

Soon we had crossed the bridge and were alive and well in the Upper Peninsula. Dad paid the toll and we crossed on to new soil. The scenery after we left Sleeping Bear had been farmland and orchards, maples and pines. But this! This place was ancient. This was awesome, raw and primitive. Cedars popped out of crumbling rock walls. Even the air felt cleaner, lighter—wilder.

I settled at the table and pulled out my new pen to write in my journal. I was going to log everything like a real explorer. What I had for lunch, when we stop for oil checks, everything—so that in two years from now I'd look back and remember. The canoe inside the pen traveled from right to left and back again, leaving the shoreline of trees. I wondered if the explorers in the old days felt excited and sad when they left their families and friends.

"So whatcha writing now?" T asked. "Can I read it?"

"Um, sure, yeah, OK," I slid my journal over to her.

"*Our goal this summer,*" read T, "*is to explore the northwestern wilderness known as the U.P.—not as in up, but as in Upper Peninsula, one of the last wild places in Michigan, or maybe the whole world. We will search for new species and discover new life while there.*"

"Yeah, Holly, Sie's right. You are weird," T joked.

"All explorers kept notes and sketches to record their journeys then compiled those in a summary," Aunt Kitty piped in. "They are very important. You forget things later if you don't write them down." I smiled.

We migrated west with the rest of the RVs, logging trucks and cars. Trees lined both sides of the road. Log cabins hid among cedars, some collapsed and deflated. We passed lumberyards with so many tall, long rows of stacked cut trees that it looked like timber trains. Pine was king here. I imagined Paul Bunyan leveling the area with one swipe of his giant ax.

After a few hours Dad chirped, "Break time!" and pulled the rig over at a gas station. "We're in Seney, home of the Seney National Wildlife Refuge."

Everyone jumped out the door to stretch or shop. Now was my chance. I had to prepare for my U.P. adventure and encounters with the natives. I wanted my first steps on Yooper soil to be in explorer mode, to do my relatives proud.

"Come *on* Holly," whined T, standing out on the pavement. "It's hot out here and I'm hungry." The twins stood with their hands on their hips.

I stepped out in my newly purchased Yooper explorer gear: I had my new bandana wrapped around my head, almost like what the voyageurs wore, and moccasins like the Indians wore, and a nifty collapsible walking stick complete with a compass and had the leather pouch from Bernie at Sleeping Bear hanging from my belt loop.

Aunt Kitty snickered, Hunter barked, the twins laughed out loud. Dad looked pale.

"I don't think I've ever seen the top of your head before," joked Sie. "It's quite a look."

"No wonder you didn't have any change left," said Dad.

"How the heck did you have enough money for all that and two bags of ice?"

"One bag," I corrected. "Wait—what? I didn't know you have to pay for ice! I thought it was free. It's water!" I felt my freckles sizzle as everyone's eyes were on me. Dad groaned softly.

"Besides, my boots were getting too small for me, they hurt my feet. And Gram said she was going to get new ones for me the next chance she had. And well, I did it for her." I wiggled my toes in my mocs for affect. "I am growing, you know, and one foot seems to grow faster than the other."

"Oh boy," Dad shook his head and smiled. "Well, we can stop and pay for the ice on our way back home." I was off the hook.

"You do look the part of an explorer," giggled Aunt Kitty. I did look really sweet. The plastic rainbow beads on my mocs shone in the sun. We walked inside for ice cream and the clerk at the counter looked me up and down like she'd never seen an explorer before.

"I-am-Holly-Wild," I said slowly and gestured to myself. "I-come-to-make-friends-and-study-your-land-and ways. We-are-going-far-to-your-Porkies." I used driving and mountain hand signs to show our journey. Sie snorted and T giggled behind me. The woman at the counter looked at me blankly.

"Will-you-accept-these-beads-in-exchange-for-ice-cream?"

I asked slowly, holding out a handful of colorful plastic beads I had gotten from a gumball machine. Sie and T were doubled over in a heap on the counter, tears running down their faces. The woman raised a penciled eyebrow.

"Cash, check or charge, honey," she said. Dad slapped some bills on the counter and grabbed me by the back of my shirt.

"Don't want our cones to melt!" he said to the lady as he pushed me out the door.

HOLLY's YOOPER Speaking Hand Signs

We drive   to   your

poky →

animal
(porcupine)

mountains

Tings Dat Go Bump in da Night

The drone of the Beast, the flapping of shades and the jangling of pots made me sleepy. I gazed out the kitchen-bedroom window at the miles upon miles of trees and dead porcupines. After counting twelve dead porkies I fell asleep.

When I woke we were in a parking lot. The twins had crashed in the back while I had slumped over my notes for a snooze on the table. I felt a little better after I woke up and looked around. In front of us the sun shone off an expanse of calm blue water.

"What's that?" I asked Aunt Kitty. Hunter was curled up next to me, snoring.

"Lake Superior," she said.

I couldn't believe my eyes! The mighty, thrashing, crashing lake of legend, the lake that swallows ore boats whole, sat there without a ripple.

"*That's* Lake Superior?" I said, rubbing my eyes.

Just then the RV's outer cabin door banged open.

"Union Bay Campground!" Dad announced through the screen door.

"Where's that?" I asked, peering out the door.

"Porcupine Mountains Wilderness State Park, of course!" he chirped. "We're here!" For a guy who was never that thrilled about nature or the outdoors he seemed pretty chipper.

I peered around Dad, expecting to see Indians in canoes and trappers in front of their cabins under towering trees, pelts drying. Instead I saw asphalt and more RVs lined up along the campground road.

"What the heck?" I blurted. "Where's the wilderness?"

Just then a shadow towered over Dad at the door. Silhouetted by the evening light stood the biggest, hairiest man I'd ever seen. He looked like a giant porcupine. Whatever hair wasn't shoved under his plaid cap burst out in every direction like a mushroom. His bristly beard glistened in the sun like it was on fire. I forgot all about wilderness.

"Hagrid?" muttered Sie, sliding on her glasses.

"Paul Bunyan?" I asked, blinking. Above his bristly beard his cheeks were speckled with freckles, and sparkly hazel eyes eyed me curiously. He wore a red plaid shirt under denim overalls which were covered in buttons. Finally! Here was an example of what I thought a Yooper would look like!

"You trolls are hardy sleepers, eh? Ya kits been here fer tirty minutes and never stirred once," the big man boomed. "Yer in Gotts country now, donchaknow."

"What did he just say?" asked T, squinting and sitting up. "Was that in English?"

"That must be Yooper talk," I said to T excitedly. I flipped open my Yooper dictionary. "He said that we children from the Lower Peninsula have been here for thirty minutes."

"Yeah, I think I get it," said Sie.

"Holly, this is Woody Timberlake," Dad interjected. "He's your cousin."

"Cousin? Wha?" I jumped up. "A real Wild in the Porky Wilderness. Awesome times ten!"

"Welcome to Michigan's largest state park!" said Woody. "Porcupine Mountains Ojibwa folks said da mountains looked like big porcupines. Dis is da place of banjo and blueberry pickin'. In a few weeks is da Porcupine Mountains Music Festival and right now is blueberry season.

"I gots a fire goin' fer youse guys over dere," he pointed. "Come on out and gib yer ol' cousin Woody a bear hug." I stood at the door and he grabbed me like a sack of taters and set me down. He grabbed hold of the twins hands and swung them to the ground. Aunt Kitty came around with water for Hunter. She looked so tiny next to Woody. It was hard to believe we were all related.

"I gots marshmellers and sodie pops over dere fer you hungry kits. Kits are always hungry, eh?" Woody guided us over to a long white RV with a sign that read CAMP HOST: WELCOME. I was still in shock.

"Are ye kits ready fer stories? I got forest stories and den I got forest stories aboot tings dat go bump in da night!" said

Woody, his eyes shining. "Kits like scary stories don't dey?"

"Heck yeah," I said. "Da scarier da better." I slapped my hand over my mouth. Holy creeps! My brain was in Yooper mode already! I didn't want him to think I was making fun of him. Fortunately, Woody didn't notice. He was busy making a s'more the size of the picnic table. The twins grabbed sodie pops from the cooler. The sun was setting and the sky was all orangey streaked and violet like taffy. The campground was settling down. I was so excited about meeting Woody I forgot all about the wilderness.

"Well, dis here tale is aboot cryptids." A dog barked in the distance. A baby cried.

"What's a cryptid?" asked Sie.

"Cryptids are hidden animals," he wiggled his fingers. "Dey live a secret life. Dese mysterious creatures are difficult to study. Most have not been proved by science. Some folks call 'em monsters. Da Porkie's own Presque Isle River is famous for Pressie. A critter like dat Loch Ness fella, donchaknow." The Team's eyes got big. Aunt Kitty giggled.

"Heh-heh. Gotta watch out for that one girls," Dad joked nervously, suddenly busying himself making a cream cheese and peanut butter s'more with chocolate, cheddar and marshmallow.

"Da udder cryptid folks talk aboot here is Bigfoot." Cheeks bulging, Dad froze mid-bite. He looked like a chipmunk who'd spotted a coyote. He even shook slightly.

"Bigfoot…" T whispered.

"Hey, Holly has big feet," joked Sie. "She had to buy moccasins because she grew out of her boots." I looked at my growing feet. They were bigger than Mom's feet or Gram's. Woody chortled at her joke.

"Surenuff dey are," Woody chuckled, his buttons hopping up and down on his britches. "Didja know dat de udder name fer

Bigfoot is Mowgli?"

"Hey, wow, Mowgli, like in the Jungle Book. I love that book," said T.

"Mowgli means Wild Man, donchaknow, eh? Well, dis Bigfoot's been known ta walk inta camps at night while folks sleep. Curious creatures dey are. Some even leave cryptic messages behind."

"Cool. Like texting?" asked Sie. Dad started scratching his neck and arms, like how I get when Ivy Buckthorn is around.

"Notes made with sticks and stones," said Aunt Kitty. "I read about that." What? Aunt Kitty reads about Bigfoot? Holy creeps! Who knew?!

"Maybe Bigfoot is the missing link," I said. Holy creeps, what if we discovered a Bigfoot or a Bigfoot discovered us?

"Who knows! Dey've been around a long time. Back in da day, ol' Daniel Boone claimed he shot hisself a Bigfoot," Woody said between crunches and crumbs. "Dey called it a Yahoo. Da Natif American folks say dat Sasquatch, or Bigfoot, is a keeper of da forest. Dere's been over four tousand sightings in da U.S. and Canada alone." Dad suddenly hopped up, dropped his s'more, spilled his pop and ran to Woody's RV.

"I n-need to—I have to—g-go—" he stammered, slamming the door.

What the heck was wrong with Dad? Before I could ask, Woody handed me a flaming marshmallow.

TIMBER TALES

There was clanging and banging going on in the RV. Dad came back out wearing a headlamp, and had a can of pepper spray and an air horn attached to his belt. He stumbled over to us and sat on his log. We all stared at him.

"Geez, Dad," I said. "What are you doing here if you're so afraid of the forest?"

"Cousin Woody has called us together to ask us for our help," Aunt Kitty explained. "We are trackers and finders of animals in the boreal forest."

"No animal too big or too small," Woody said proudly. "We track and tag dose in need of help. Our motto is 'Fett'ered or furred, we find our friends', donchaknow,"

"Wait," I said, looking at Dad shaking on his log. "*You're* a tracker? But you're terrified of the outdoors!"

"I'm n-not called Wolff for n-nothing, you know," Dad said through chattering teeth.

"Your dad grew up in the woods," Aunt Kitty explained, "and was an accomplished tracker by the age of twelve."

Holy Creeps! Wild secrets times 10!

"What are you tracking?" asked Sie.

"Oh, well, bats…." Woody said.

"Bats?! How do you track bats?" I demanded.

"Oh, um, you look for their guano in caves," Aunt Kitty said. "The Porkies contain important bat habitat, and we are going to get information about their population."

"And dere's da lynxes, donchaknow!" Woody added. "Dere a rare critter in dese parts dat we want to know more aboot."

I looked at Dad, still suspicious. "So, what happened to make you so afraid of the outdoors?" I asked.

Just then a tall young girl, silent and dark as a shadow, appeared. In glasses, short dark hair, wearing a black hoodie, shorts and sandals, she slithered over by Aunt Kitty.

"Oh hey, Marley!" said Woody. "Dis here is Marley Soyle, yer camp counselor."

"OUR WHAT?" the Team and I yelped. Marley waggled her pinky at us, smiling as crooked as the glasses tilting on her face.

"Woody started a camp and needs campers," explained Aunt Kitty. "That's where you will be while we go out tracking."

"Wait," I said. "We're going *WHERE*?"

"The film crew for the TV show *Critter Country* is in town to film Woody's camp as part of a segment on the Porkies," Aunt Kitty continued. "Because the camp is so new no one was signed up yet, so we volunteered you three."

"I need youse kits fer a week," said Woody. "I talked to Gypsy Rose, and she says she got da kits, and I need kits to make da camp look good. I got a couple of other kits comin' in tomorrow."

"Wait, Gram knew about this?! What happened to Dad-daughter time?" I howled. "Besides, I came here to camp out, not *go* to camp!" I looked at him open-mouthed.

"Woody needs us, sweetheart. It'll be good for you. Besides, you owe me," He winked and patted his wallet. "You can put your new gear to use."

When I didn't think it could possibly get any weirder, up walked Misty Hills, T and Sie's mom, in her long flowing multi-colored skirt with a flower in her hair.

"My chickadees!" Mrs. Hills called, her arms open wide.

"MOM!" The twins charged over to her and gave her a squeeze that nearly sent her backwards into the fire. We forgot all about her being here with all of the squatch hubbub.

"Hi Mrs. Hills," I said. She came over and gave me a squeeze too. "That's from your mother," she winked.

Coyotes started up their yipping song in the wooded hills above the campground.

"De kiyoots are saying da party is over. Time ta hit da hay." Woody slapped his thigh and got up. "Gotta put on da Joe in the morn fer da early risers." Aunt Kitty, Hunter and Dad climbed into Woody's RV while the Team and I with Mrs. Hills slept in the Beast. Mrs. Hills slept on the table bed, the twins slept in back and I got my bunk. Marley had her own tent.

"Mom, can't we stay with you for your artist thing?" asked Sie. "Please?"

"Sorry, honey," said Mrs. Hills. "Rules are that only the artist stays at the cabin. No kids allowed."

Somewhere in the distance there was a rumble like thunder and the cry of some creature.

Say ya to da U.P., eh?

Day 2 (Monday)

Camp Firewood For Sale

Morning came early. With the shock and news of yesterday over, the new day held the promise of adventure. Heck, camp may not be so bad and learning new camp skills is exciting. Who knows, our party may even catch a glimpse of a legendary Pressie or Bigfoot.

I snapped my journal shut and was basking in the glory of being in the bunk when I noticed the Team looking glum. I waved and slipped my Yooper bandana on. Sie rolled her eyes.

"I still don't understand why we have to go to a camp when a perfectly good RV is sitting right here," said Sie. Mrs. Hills had already been up and made her bed back into a dining table again. There was a wild rose in a mug in the middle. Cereal, little bowls and spoons waited for us. Aw. Mom stuff.

I heard talking outside and went to the door to listen.

Standing around the fire were the adults.

"Camp Firewood fer sale it read," said Woody, "so I went in to inquire. I always wanted a camp fer kits. Camp reminds me of my days of yoot, living in da lumber camp. I wanted a camp to show lil kits tings my mama taught me. How to track, cook, and chop trees."

Woody slurped his coffee. Aunt Kitty listened intently, sipping her tea. "'Is dis here Camp Firewood really for sale?'" I asked him. "'Yep, sure shootin','" says he, "'Den, hot diggety, I'll take it all,' 'I says, "'lock, stock and barrel. Da whole shebang. Cabins, out buildings, fire pit and dose cords of stick wood and all dose logs ya got dere, eh? All I got is my life's savings. Will dat cover it?'"

Dad's and Aunt Kitty's eyes met. Dad shook his head—he could see where this was going.

Woody continued. "'Sir, I don't tink you understand,' he says. 'I sell campfire woo—say how much is yer life savings, anyways?' he says. I tink he was a tad bit choked up on giving up da camp." Woody winked at us. "I got a good deal on 'er. Two hunert t'ousand smackers and dat's how I got my dream camp."

Dad slapped his forehead. Aunt Kitty looked away and cleared her throat.

"Last I heard he and da missus moofed out for big city life of Germfask. I fixed up da cabins and patched up some tents I found. So I say ta maself, now dat I have a camp, how do I run it? I know lumber, I know timber but I don't know kits. So dat's why I got Marley here fresh outta college to help run it. Cook grub, teach da kits and take 'em hiking."

In the RV we quietly packed our gear. I hugged Dad goodbye and the twins hugged their mom goodbye. Marley and

Aunt Kitty shoved our gear into the back of a huge, banged up, timber-striped van with the Camp Firewood logo on the door and we were off. On our way out of the Union Bay Campground we saw a giant black RV with bicycles propped against it.

"The Death Star," muttered T. "It seems to be following us everywhere we go."

My freckles began to twitch and itch.

We pulled up to the camp just outside the Porcupine Mountains' eastern border. Marley parked near the door, and we carried our stuff inside.

"This is it, Camp Firewood," she said, tossing her keys on the counter and slumping onto a chair.

"You have a class at eleven and then lunch. Then we are hiking to Lake of the Clouds. The bunkhouse is over there— go choose your bunk. Dinner at five, quiet time at eight." She pointed at the chalkboard schedule on the wall next to shelves of dusty faded books.

We dragged our bags into the attached bunkhouse.

"It looks like an old barn, and smells like sweaty, dirty socks in here," said T, holding her nose.

It did seem a little rugged and raw, but hey, that's the U.P. At least we had first dibs on bunks. Light shone through a hole in the ceiling, and under it someone had put a bucket. There was a large door at the far end and straw in the corners. Maybe it *was* a barn at one time.

"Isn't this cool?" I said, looking around. Acorns were strewn across the cement floor, spiders crept into dark corners, the smell of skunk and pine filled the air. No wonder Marley wanted this job. It was U.P. heaven.

T and Sie looked forlorn. Sie grabbed a broom and started sweeping. T organized her clothes and placed them into a rickety old dresser drawer.

"Good thing there hasn't been rain here in a while," Sie said, inspecting the bucket.

I hung my new old backpack and clothes on a hook on an upper bunk by a filthy, cracked window. I hopped up there, opened my sleeping bag and laid out my pillow. Ah, this was the life.

Just then a deafening rumbling roar of something like a jet engine, and voices floated into the bunkhouse. T and Sie walked over to the door to sneak a peek. I crawled out of my comfy perch to join them. Through a crack in the timber wall we could see the Death Star RV parked out front, and we could hear Marley giving someone the Camp Firewood talk.

"Remember that a hundred eyes watch you as you walk the forest," she said, leaning over the counter with a clipboard in hand. "The Porcupine Mountains Wilderness State Park has over 60,000

acres for you guys to get lost in. I wouldn't suggest it cuz there are wolves and things that can eat you." Suddenly there was a squeal of terror.

"A gerbil just ran into the cabin!" squeaked an excited voice.

"That's a chipmunk, not a gerbil," said Marley. Then the kid bobbed around the counter and stopped in the doorway to look wide-eyed at us, and puffed on an inhaler.

"Hey! It's that boy from the Wilderness State Park. The one on the bike with the dreadlocks!" T reported. I edged closer to see the others.

"The Porkies, as we call it, was made a State Park in 1945 and then a Wilderness Area in the 1970's to protect it from mining, logging and other development," Marley continued.

"Boring," came a nasally, screechy voice, like fingers raking a chalkboard. I really, really, really times ten hoped it did not belong to the blond girl with icy eyes as cold as Lake Superior who we'd seen with Dread-head Boy. As I moved closer I caught the rain bucket on my foot and it clanged loudly. I tripped and flew into the office past the desk and across the floor.

"Strudelberry Snotcake!" I heard an all-too familiar voice guffaw. I did not want to look up. There is only one person in the world who calls me names like that. Ivy Buckthorn. Now the U.P. is a pretty dang big place. What are the chances, really? I slowly got up, the bucket still caught and clanging, my freckles sizzling hot and faced my foe.

Ivy snickered. "What's the haps, brats? Long time no smell. Looks like we're bunkies," she said, rolling her suitcase past us into the bunkhouse. Standing next to the boy in dreads was the girl with icy eyes. A slow evil grin spread across her face. Lovely times three, donchaknow.

GAME OF WILDERNESS SURVIVAL

"OK, plantigrades, hop to it," Marley said. She picked up her clipboard and walked to the office door.

"Planting what? Huh?" asked Dread-head Boy.

"Plantigrades are animals that walk flat-footed. Humans, bears, raccoons," said Marley. "Unload your gear and report out front in ten." She walked outside with her cell phone in hand.

I was still in shock and pretty filthy from my fall. Icy Girl dragged her stuff over my feet and into the bunkroom.

"I'm taking the bunk by the window. Top side," she said without cracking a grin or grimace.

"That's my bunk! It's all set up. There's others over there," I pointed and unhooked the bucket from my foot.

"Yeah, well," she screeched, "They aren't this one." She yanked my sleeping bag down. Then Sie jumped in.

"Hey look girlie, that's my friend's bunk. Take another," she said. Sie and Icy Girl stood staring each other down. Icy Girl was much smaller than Sie and kinda hefty. T suddenly broke the silence and walked up to Icy girl.

"I'm Tierra Hills, pleased to meet you," T said, thrusting out her hand. "This is my sister, Sierra. That is Holly, our friend," Icy stared at her.

"I'm Viola Vetch," her voice scratched. "Welcome to my

camp. This is my bunk." T backed away. Dread-head Boy walked over to Viola.

"C-come on, cut her some slack, Vi," he said. He turned to us. "I'm Martin Fisher, the Third. Pleased to meet you." He smiled and limply shook my hand and T's. Sie and Viola were still glaring at each other. Finally Viola gave a tiny sigh and moved her stuff across the room. She sat on a bunk staring at us. I was glad that was over. I stuffed my bag back up into my bunk.

"Creepy," T whispered to me. Martin and Ivy set up their camp across the room, too.

Marley blew a whistle outside and we filed out to where she stood. She held her clipboard and waited for us to join her.

"OK, like this is what's going down. We're going to play a game." Oh, good that would certainly break the tenseness of the situation. Even though we actually made art with Ivy back in Sleeping Bear, I still did not like being in the same room with her. Now with this new Vetch girl, I was even more uncomfortable.

"So, who here has watched that TV show, *'Sole Survival'*? It's where people have to live on rice and dirt and bugs." We all raised our hands.

"Our game is called Wilderness Survival. There will be challenges, clan councils, points given for winning and good conduct and points taken away for poor conduct. Then we will head back to the bunkhouse to make macaroni crafts because that's all the grocery store had." She nervously tapped her clipboard with her pen.

"You will be learning about the four things you need to survive in the wilderness. This is the wilderness, so it's vital to know these things and know your teammates," said Marley. "By the end of the week we will see who has 'Persisted, Prolonged and Persevered.' Any questions?" Martin raised his hand. Marley waggled her pen at him.

"Can I just look those words up right now?" he pulled out his cell phone to check the words, "I've got an app for that." Right then a dragonfly hovered near him and Martin freaked out, screamed and dropped to the ground. But then he saw a bug crawling on the ground and jumped back up, thrashing the air wildly.

"Bugs! No one said that there'd be bugs here! I even put on spray just in case." The Team and I looked at him. Clearly he had puffed his inhaler one too many times. There's a limit on how often you can use those things, donchaknow. Marley waited for him to calm down. Ivy snorted and Viola stared at me.

"OK, eco-challengers, are you ready for races, memory challenges and puzzles?" Everyone nodded. How bad could it be really? "Good," Marley said. "We'll now pick our teams."

Ivy announced loudly, "My team name is team S.P.O.R.K.,

the Society of Privileged Overachiever Rich Kids. That was the name my mom gave to us before we got here."

I announced louder, "My team is Team Wild, we are GeEKS, Geo-explorer Kids," I added for affect, pointing out T and Sie.

"Hold your horses campers, nature is picking the team for you," Marley said, pulling out a grocery sack. "In this bag I have pine cones, our state's official tree the white pine. I painted some red and some blue. Whatever color you pick is the team you are on. No trading. The pine shall speak for your team."

I felt faint. I didn't care less if it was red, white or blue pine. My hand shook, my freckles bounced. I shut my eyes and pulled out a blue cone. Ivy pulled a red. Whew! Then T pulled a red. I started to sweat. Then Martin pulled a blue. Well, at least Martin seemed pretty nice for a privileged overachiever rich kid.

It came down to the last two. Sie pulled a red cone, which left blue for Viola.

Poor Sie and T were stuck with Ivy but at least they had each other. My heart pounded as Viola walked over to Martin and me, her hair bouncing as her icy laser eyes burned holes into my soul. I tried to inspect flower pollen on my boot or ants or whatever my eyes could focus on that was not her. I'd never felt so alone.

Marley went on, oblivious to my plight. "Survival, by definition, is the struggle or ability to remain alive. In the wilderness,

CONE OF UNLUCKINESS

there are four important things for survival: Air, shelter, water and food. In that order. You can go four minutes without air, four hours without shelter, depending on weather, four days without water, and four weeks without food." I heard chowhound T gasp at that one. I was wondering how I was going to survive four days without my team. I was alone with a whimpering puppy and a rabid wild dog.

"We will work on air later today when you will hike to Lake of the Clouds. Yes, Martin, you can use your inhaler. The first challenge will be to build a shelter. The forest is your survival friend. Everything you need to survive is in the forest."

We nodded weakly.

"On my count the two teams, GEEK and SPORK, will race to make a shelter. Use teamwork and your imagination and use whatever you find lying around." That actually sounded kinda fun. Forts were my specialty.

"Make a really cool shelter and win a reward of extra dessert. We will have lunch a little late so you have plenty of time to work." She then blew her whistle and sat in a lawn chair in the cool shade.

Off we went, Martin running like a seal on dry land, Viola waddling like a duck. Gram had said to listen to the trees. So I went there first. I raced to find branches, birch bark and ferns, moss, lichens and logs. Martin kicked pine needles and sand into a pile. while I sorted sticks. I turned to look to see where Viola was. She stood in front of the office waving at something. Good grief. Survival would not come easy with this new team.

"What gives? Why aren't you helping?" I yelled at Vi. She turned and glared at me.

"OK, Martin, tuck these small sticks and grasses in the cracks," I said as I leaned big branches up against a tree like a giant cone. He wheezed and collapsed from exhaustion. I placed ferns over the sticks. I didn't have time to check out my old Team's teamwork. There stood Vi by the office, still coldly staring at me.

"Hey, what's the deal with Viola?" I asked Martin, whose

breathing sounded like a snoring beagle. I thought it best to be friendly and learn information that may come in handy. Survival was the name of this week's game and I needed all the help I could get.

"V-Vi's pretty strange. I-I really don't know her," he said wheezing. "I try to stay away from b-both of them."

"How do you know Ivy? The last time I saw her she was in an ambulance with her folks, headed to Traverse City."

"Well, actually, that's where we picked her up," Martin said. "We had another kid with us but he got s-sick so I guess they ran into Ivy at the hospital. Her parents seemed eager to ship her off."

"So then why are you here?" I asked.

"I had no choice," Martin wheezed. "My uncle is a cameraman on the *Critter Country* film crew. He told my mom the fresh air would help my asthma." He shrugged. "Viola's mom's a producer for the show. Viola is really mean. Can I be your f-friend?" He pleaded with me with his big brown eyes.

"Yeah, sure," I smiled. "Let's finish."

"I'm afraid I'll get a rash," he said, and coughed. So I finished. We stood up and looked at our efforts. Viola was no longer standing by the office.

We finally looked at Team SPORK's shelter. They had put up a six by six Day-Glo orange backpacking tent with inflatable cushions neatly arranged inside. T and Sie looked sadly at me while Ivy grinned. They had made a mailbox from an old lunchbox with a little flag for clan mail. I boiled inside. Marley smiled from ear to ear and walked over to where Viola stood. We all followed.

"Viola, is it?" asked Marley. "Is your team finished?" I looked at Martin. He was holding his cell phone up, trying to get a good signal.

"*Her* team? She didn't do anything!" I retorted. Marley ignored me.

"Where is your shelter Viola?" Marley asked again. Vi silently pointed her finger like the grim reaper at the camp office door.

"I was taking care of a problem," she said cryptically.

"What problem, Viola?" asked Marley. Just then Ivy and the SPORKS started running and screaming. I looked in time to see angry black hornets buzzing out of my shelter. I pushed the gasping Martin out of the way and he ran. Vi had tossed a hornet's honeycombed nest into our shelter and they were none too happy.

Vi walked calmly away as I danced about trying to knock the nest out into the woods with a stick, then losing my balance I fell into the fort, knocking half of it to the ground, but not before getting stung in two places.

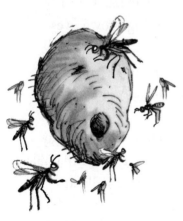

"Holly, what are you doing?" Sie yelled, alarmed. Ivy snickered. Marley looked at Martin and I, displeased. Hands and clipboard on her hip, she tapped her foot. T ran for ice.

"This is not funny, guys. You were clearly given directions to prepare a shelter. And you endangered the camp with your games. GEEKS lose. Team SPORK wins."

"Um, but Martin and I made a real shelter, not a store bought one," I pleaded. But it was too late, everyone else was filing in for lunch.

"Sorry, Holly," T said, handing me the ice. My leg and arm hurt from the stings. The hornet sting was not as bad as seeing my Team with Ivy on the other side.

"Oh, and by the way GEEKs, no electronics allowed," Marley said. "Five points for Team SPORK. Put it away or I take it away." Martin gulped and put his phone in his pocket. Marley looked at me like I knew better. I don't even have a phone.

Persist, Prolong, Persevere. This week was turning out to be a real game of survival and I, Holly H. Wild, was on my own.

HAPPY CAMPERS

UNHAPPY CAMPERS

"This part of the building used to be a sugar shack for making maple syrup," Marley said, passing out sack lunches. I was starving. We opened the bags in front of us. Grapes, blueberries and walnuts and dried leaves rolled out. The single flower sitting in the middle of the table was looking pretty good right now. I couldn't imagine what Team SPORK's dessert would be. Cabbage?

"Excuse me," I said, dumping mine into a colorful pile. "I think I got one of the dessert bags by mistake."

"Nope, that's your lunch," Marley said, popping a grape into her mouth.

"It looks like a squirrel bait pile to me," Ivy bellowed. "Where's the meat, you know, bologna, cheese, gravy?"

"There's not any juice box or pop. No chips, cookie or candy bars," Martin whined, feeling deeper into the paper sack.

My stomach growled big time. I thought a Yooper lunch would be pasties and pancakes, not nature stuff. My morning cereal had not lasted long. Suddenly a vision of the crunchewy, chocomallow granola bar hidden in my backpack popped into my head and refused to leave.

Marley smiled at us. "Survival," she said proudly. Her pale skin glowed in the dark, cheerless room. "You should be glad! This is a real treat. You're eating *organic* stuff vegan style. Eat up campers."

"Is dirt organic?" asked Martin, holding his leaf out like it was poison ivy.

"What's up with the fried lettuce?" asked Ivy, crumbling hers into powder.

"Those are kale chips," said Marley, nibbling on her own. "They are baked, not fried. Try one, they're good for you."

Broccoli--
the NOT Yooper
FOOD!

Ivy crunched nuts loudly and open-mouthed. Sie sorted piles of fruit in order by size. Martin chased his grapes around the table. But Viola, who sat staring across from me, slowly picked up each grape, stuck it between her teeth and popped the skins.

"Vegan? I thought that was a religion," I whispered to Sie. She smiled and eyed her pile of blueberries. This was truly going to be a struggle for survival.

I ate my meager lunch pile. I was glad our team lost when I saw Marley bring out dessert. More kale chips. T and Sie looked blankly at their pile of dark green crumbles.

"Extra kale chips. You'll thank me later," Marley said. No wonder the girl was so skinny. She ate like a vegan mouse. My stomach growled again.

"After lunch you have an hour of free time. There is a library in the office with some books on lumbering, the history of the Porcupine Mountains and guidebooks on plants. Help yourself." I turned around and noticed that Viola and Martin were gone. Probably went back to get whatever junk food stash they brought with them. Now was my chance to go grab my survival granola bar.

I went in to the bunkroom and Martin lay on his bunk with

headphones plugged in, playing his cell phone video game. Viola sat up straight on her bunk, staring. Time to get to know the enemy, make them feel at ease.

"So Viola," I said, finally getting the nerve to look her in the eye. "Do you like camping?" She gave me a blank, slow, creepy smile like a snake uncoiling. I guess this meant to leave her alone. She picked up a book next to her on Zombies and totally ignored me.

I climbed up to my bunk to find a pile of bitten grapes, nut shells, and an empty torn granola wrapper in my sleeping bag. I turned back and found Vi staring at me.

"Why did you do that?" I got down and went over to her, my freckles flaming.

"Do what?" her gravelly voice grated.

"You know, put fruit on my bed, eat my granola bar. That!"

"I don't like you," she said and went back to reading. Sie came over with T.

"You don't know if she did it," Sie said, pulling me away.

"Martin was in here, too."

"Whatever," I said, "I'm keeping a close eye on her." This was about survival. And not having my granola bar meant sure starvation and extreme crabbiness.

"We're going to the library," T said. "Why don't you come with us?"

"Maybe there's a good recipe book on weeds," joked Sie. That made me feel a bit better. Maybe we *were* still secretly a Team.

We rifled through books on first aid, deer hunting, ticks, timbering, guidebooks on rocks, and old novels. No kid books. But the book on Porcupine Mountains history caught my eye. So I went outside with that and flipped through it.

After our break Marley blew her whistle.

"Campers," she announced. "Grab your water bottles and gear. We're hiking." At last! I could use my nifty hiking stick that I got back in Mackinaw City. I snapped it open in one mighty movement.

"Awesome," Martin said, his eyes bugging.

"There's no better way to get acquainted with your tribe members than by an invigorating afternoon hike." Marley said. We piled into the Camp Firewood van.

"This afternoon we will hike to the Summit Peak Overlook where you'll get to see a bird's eye view of the park. Then we will drive over to the famous Lake of the Clouds, where you will have your second challenge."

After a half mile walk we climbed the observation tower for a panoramic view of the park. Marley read from her clipboard.

"The Porcupine Mountains are not officially mountains anymore. To be considered a mountain, a peak must be at least 2,000 feet. Summit Peak is the highest peak in the Porkies at 1,958 feet. Due to erosion and sliding over time, the Porkies have shrunk."

"Kinda like my grandma," snorted Ivy.

Marley shot Ivy a look, then continued: "The rock that makes up the mountains was formed 1.1 billion years ago—"

"It's almost as old as my grandma, too," Ivy murmured.

"—and are made up primarily of basalt, rhyolite, conglomerate and sandstone." Marley tucked her clipboard under her arm.

"Looks like dragon skin," said T, looking down over the side of the tower.

"Like you've seen dragon skin," Ivy said. "I thought all rock is old, like dinosaurs."

"There are lots of different kinds of rock here at the Porkies," explained Marley. "We'll see different kinds when we hit the beach later this week."

By the time we drove back to Lake of the Clouds we were already tired, and Martin was wheezing.

"The Lake of the Clouds is up that trail," Marley said, pointing. "Most tourists walk up, strike some ridiculous pose, snap a photo and then leave. Today we aren't doing that. We are going to *race* up, pose and come back." We groaned.

I slipped on my bandana, Sie checked her camera batteries and T tightened her hair bobs.

"This is Challenge Mode Oxygen. We all need air, so we will expand our lungs by racing up the mountain, which is not technically a mountain," Marley instructed. "Then you'll come back down. The first team back will win more dessert tonight." The Team and I, which was not my Team, looked at each other. Ivy pulled out a thermometer and a GPS. The GPS blipped and flashed, ready to read to her where we were.

"I thought we couldn't use electronic devices," I said.

"In the mountains, they come in handy," she said. "You should learn to use one." I sighed.

52

I wondered if dessert was a carrot stick. I was already feeling lightheaded. I looped my walking stick around my wrist. I took a compass reading. Well, the needle pointed north anyway. Actually, I don't know how to use a compass but it looks cool and telling someone that you're taking a compass reading is even cooler. I'd have to work on this.

Marley blew her whistle and off we went. T and Sie ran and Ivy followed behind.

"Slow and steady wins the race," I told Martin, who was soon having a rough time. His water bottle and inhaler dangled and clanged from his belt. By the time we arrived at the halfway point he had hit his inhaler a second time. Marley must have trusted that none of us would fall off the cliff since she was back in the van.

By the time we reached the top, Ivy and Team SPORK were on their way down. I was furious. I kept waiting for Martin but Viola was nowhere to be seen.

At the top I helped Martin to the ledge and dropped his water bottle into my backpack. We gazed a moment at the blueness of the lake and the expanse of trees.

"The mountains do look like porcupines," I said.

"Where?" cried Martin, his dreads waggling about as he frantically searched. "No one told me that there would be wild porcupines here!"

"There aren't any right here right now. The Indians said the mountains *looked* like porcupines." I said, sketching the trees. "See how poky the trees are on top? I bet that's why. The trees are the quills on the rock porcupine's back." I pretended my pack was a porcupine and I lumbered around hunched over to make him laugh.

"Then the lake must be their drool," joked Martin.

Suddenly there came a cry of pain, shrill and loud. Martin and I started down the trail. Ivy lay crumpled on the ground as Viola calmly walked past her.

"My knee, it's bleeding!" Ivy snarled. "That creepy Viola brat jumped out of the bushes and tripped me!"

T pulled out a first aid kit and Sie applied a bandage to her wound. Martin and I helped her up. Ivy had

fire in her eyes. I think she had met her match.

"That demon kid has no idea who she's messing with." Ivy limped down the trail. Martin and the Team and I followed.

When we got to the parking lot, Marley pulled off her headphones and grinned. "Beautiful up there isn't it?" Viola stepped up and tagged Marley and stopped. "Finish," she said.

Marley saw Ivy half-hobbling and half marching toward her. "Looks like Team GEEK wins this one." Ivy was outraged and the girls moaned in protest.

"But Vi cheated!" Sie said, pointing at us. "She didn't even make it to the top! Then she tripped Ivy on our way back."

"But I was helping Martin!" I said. "We even stopped to help Ivy back onto her feet." But Marley ignored me as Ivy showed her her scraped knee and whimpered pathetically.

"Well then," Marley announced, "ten points taken away from Team GEEK for unsportswomanly conduct. Points and reward go to SPORK." Martin and I groaned. I glared at Vi.

"Tomorrow we go waterfall watching. Persist, Prolong and Persevere," said Marley, tapping her clipboard. "And these GEEK jokes need to stop." This was not fair. We didn't all cheat.

After dinner, team SPORK got their just desserts—carrot juice. I was beginning to think that Cousin Woody would be a better camp counselor than Marley Soyle.

BATS IN CAMP

After the long day, we sat around in the bunkhouse for After Dinner Free Time. Hungry, hornet stung, and broken, it would have been more fun to cut and stack firewood than spend the day like we did.

"How about a spooky story? You tell really good stories Holly," T suggested. I only had enough energy to sigh loudly. Sie rolled her eyes and shut her book.

Then Marley came in and broke the uncomfortable silence, whistling and tapping her clipboard.

"First night in camp can be rough for campers. Here at Camp Firewood we want happy campers. It was a long day so Clan Council time will be a little different. In order to keep idle hands busy and fill sleeping minds with good dreams, we are going to make dreamcatchers. The dreamcatcher is to put over your bunk so you won't have bad dreams."

"Geez, we did those back in second grade out of stupid paper plates," Ivy complained. But Martin's eyes lit up. It was the look of hope. A shield to keep bad things at bay!

Marley looked at her stack of paper plates and started to hide them behind her back. Then she shrugged and handed them to us anyway. We followed Marley into the dining area to work on our dreamcatchers.

We cut out a donut-sized hole in the center and punched holes in a circle on them before stringing rainbow yarn through the holes and tying on colored macaroni. As a last thought Marley pulled out red, green and yellow spotted craft feathers for us. Ivy's dreamcatcher ended up looking like a parrot ran into it. Viola's was a paper plate with yarn and macaroni glued into a pile in the center—it looked like a macaroni salad. T's was creatively collaged and Sie's turned out better than Marley's example. Mine was a gluey feathery beady smudged lump and my hands were too. Martin already had taken his to his bunk to hang.

"There, that should do the trick for the night," Marley said, checking her clipboard. After she said goodnight, she clicked off the lights and went to her room through a door marked Private.

"So you wanted spooky stories huh?" a scratchy voice pierced the dark. T cleared her throat. Martin whimpered in his corner.

"I don't think so. Pretty late," said Sie.

"M-maybe not too scary. Maybe about porcupines or hornets," Martin suggested, his teeth chattering.

"I'm a vampire," Viola said.

"Ha," snorted Ivy. "Does that mean you sleep hanging upside down?"

"No, it means that I drink blood. Like bats. And tonight is a full moon." With that statement Martin hit the floor in terror and sprinted out the door into the moonlit night.

T and Sie ran after him while Vi ran screeching and laughing into the night. This was Ivy's big chance. Like a predator/prey trigger where the rabbit runs and the coyote

chases, Ivy was out the door after Vi. I sat on my bunk and sighed. Marley burst through the door, her glasses on sideways, in her Sponge Bob robe.

"Campers?" she yelled, scanning the empty room.

"They all took off. Viola announced that she is a vampire. Martin freaked out. Ivy is—hunting." Marley took off out the door and followed the shrieks into the woods. I slid off my bunk. I may as well see the outcome for myself.

I stepped out into the hazy, eerie, full moonlit camp. Sounds traveled in from all directions. Sobs, moans and cries filled the night air. I had to resort to tracking them by ear.

"Marco!" I yelled.

"Polo," Sie answered from the shadows. It was our quick Team Wild location system.

"Marco," I yelled again.

"Yoo-OOP!" came a reply from deep in the woods.

I jumped when Sie grabbed my shoulder. "What the heck was THAT?" she whispered. T appeared at my other shoulder.

"I don't know," I said, shaking, "but it sounded BIG."

"What if it was a wolf?!" T exclaimed.

"Where's Martin?" asked Sie, panic in her voice.

We were relieved to find Martin curled up on the ground in the parking lot, next to the Camp Firewood van. Marley was busy keeping Vi and Ivy apart. The big overhead light had all kinds of cool moths dancing around it.

"I want to go home," Martin whimpered. "I saw her turn into a bat. I don't want to be bitten by a bat or a vampire girl." T comforted him by handing him some gorp.

"Martin, bats do not drink blood," Marley explained. "Michigan has nine different species of bats and all of them eat insects—no blood."

"They do?" he croaked.

"Yes, the very insects that you are afraid of, they eat like thousands of those in one night." Marley said, close to losing her cool. She turned to Viola.

"Why did you tell your campmates that you are a vampire, Vi?" Marley asked. Vi shrugged her shoulders.

"Because vampires are cool." Vi wore a tiny wicked smile with a strange glint in her ice blue eyes. I think there was more to it than that.

"Whatever, drama Dracula queen," Ivy snorted. "I'm heading back. You twerps can hang out here. I got Z's to catch before tomorrow's hike. Later, losers." Ivy marched back inside.

Martin was still shaking. "I don't want them in my hair," he whimpered. "With hair like mine I know they're just waiting to get tangled up in it and bite me."

Marley looked like she was ready to pull *her* hair out. Running a camp for kids was *nothing* like college.

"That's not true, that's a myth," she said. "Bats don't get tangled in your hair. They have super sonar powers and they can tell the difference between a bug and a person."

"Why do there have to be bats, anyway?" Martin asked.

"Bats save the country billions of dollars every year just by eating crop and forest damaging insects," Marley said, pushing us back inside. "That's why the old mines and caves here in the U.P. are important—they are places for bats to hibernate. Right now it's time for you bats to hit the belfry and go to sleep."

"Bats still creep me out. Where I live I don't go out at night and actually not much during the day," said Martin. "We don't have nature where I live."

"Well, if you learn about something you won't be afraid of it," Sie said.

Chapter 10

Day 3 (Tuesday)
Big Carbon Footprint

After our breakfast of fruits and nuts we started getting ready for the arrival of the film crew. Sie organized the books in the library, arranging them by theme alphabetically. T hung up a Porcupine Mountains map on the wall. She placed red tacks on Lake of the Clouds and Summit Peak, where we had been. Martin drew a cool map of Camp Firewood.

We went outside to find stuff to make a North Woods centerpiece for the lunchroom table. We gathered spruce branches, moss and pine cones. It was real teamwork, and I forgot all about the "game" for a while.

"I hope we have lumberjack pasties for lunch," I said.

"Pancakes," corrected Sie. "Lumberjacks ate pancakes or flap jacks. Miners ate pasties."

"OK, either way I'm starving," I said.

"Hey, look what I found," croaked Vi, dangling a toad by its tiny leg.

"Awesome find, Viola," Marley said. "But be careful, we don't want to hurt it. He can be the highlight of the centerpiece, but just for today. We will release him tonight."

We didn't have pasties *or* pancakes for lunch. Instead we

had what Marley called a "forest meal"—sautéed mushrooms on pasta, (the pasta, she said, would be like the inner bark of a white pine tree, which you could eat if you were starving), nuts and blueberries. It was surprisingly good.

After lunch we were having a Clan Council gathering around the fire pit when Woody, Dad and Mrs. Hills rolled up in the Beast. I wanted to run up and beg them to save me, but I didn't want to hurt Woody's feelings.

"Are you kits ready fer yer big day on TV?" Woody asked, clapping his hands and smiling.

"We were just getting ready to discuss energy and carbon footprints," beamed Marley. Ivy sighed and rolled her eyes.

"Oooo, footprints! That sounds exciting!" Woody exclaimed. "Do you track them?"

Right then the Death Star RV rolled in, followed by an SUV.

"Well there's a big carbon footprint right there," Marley said.

The crew of the *Critter Country* TV show climbed out of the RV. The large, Wookie-like guy who we'd seen at the Wilderness campground got out first, followed by a fancy-looking woman wearing very clean safari-type clothing and lots of jewelry.

Behind her was a nervous, skinny guy dressed in a jogging suit who looked completely out of place in a wilderness area. A man in a baseball cap with a goatee got out of the SUV.

"There's my uncle!" Martin whispered to me, and waved.

Woody brought the crew over to meet us.

"Kits, dis here is Howler,"

Woody said, pointing to Wookiee-guy. "He puts the 'Critter' in *Critter Country*. He can hoot like an owl and fight like a bear." Howler let out a hoot like a foghorn.

"Dis purdy lady here is Verna, da hostess and director of da show." Verna stood with her arms crossed, looking bored and impatient.

I elbowed Sie in the ribs. "Hey, Martin told me that's Viola's mom!" I whispered.

Before Sie could reply, the skinny guy in the jogging suit pushed to the front of the group, waving his hands in the air.

"Hey there, I'm Buzz!" he exclaimed, taking off his mirrored sunglasses. "Are you children having a good time? Oh that's super! Super, yeah, awesome!" he said before any of us could answer.

"OK!" said Woody. "Last, dat feller over dere is Laser, the cameraman." Laser was busy setting up equipment.

Woody spread his arms wide. "Dis here is Camp Firewood. I'll give youse da grand tour," he beamed.

"No thank you, Mr. Timberlake," droned Verna. "We can find our way around. OK people, time is money. Let's set up this shot."

We sat in our clan council circle with Marley. She held a stick with cones, shells and macaroni dangling from it, which she called a talking stick. Only the person holding the stick was allowed to speak, she explained. It had to be passed back and forth if you wanted to answer a question or discuss things.

"We are going to talk about energy," Marley said as the camera rolled, "and our carbon footprint."

"What is a carbon foot print exactly?" asked Martin.

"I'm getting to that, Martin," said Marley, shaking the stick at him. "The energy we use emits greenhouse gases that cause climate change."

"Oh yeah, burping cows belching holes into the sky," said Ivy, emitting her own belch into the atmosphere.

"No, that's the ozone layer," corrected Marley sharply. "And excuse you, Ivy," she said and shook the talking stick again. "Cows do belch methane which is also a greenhouse gas. But it's our use of energy that I want to talk about. It's home heating and cooling. It's lights, clocks, cell phone chargers, music players and computers being left on. It's the production of food. It's the burning of coal, oil and gas to produce the electricity we use. Each one of us makes a carbon footprint. We need to make that print as small as possible." We all looked at our feet. My left foot was growing larger than my right.

"Growing food uses energy. Raising cattle for meat uses a lot more energy than growing vegetables—in addition to methane burps, cows eat a lot of grains that use a lot of energy to grow. That's why we're eating organic fresh fruits, veggies and nuts. They're good for you and for the earth."

"I did like the nuts we had," said Ivy. "Tasted like chicken, less greasy."

"It's like crunching bones," Vi smirked.

"But wait, you still have to do the dishes, and refrigerate the food," said Sie.

"And wash the dish towels," said T.

"A—hem!" Marley cleared her throat loudly and waved the talking stick at us.

"We could all line dry, like we did in Empire," I said.

"Even our clothes use energy to be made!" exclaimed Martin, his dreads bouncing.

"Don't forget vacations," said Ivy. "Gas for cars—and just making the cars!"

Marley looked sadly at the talking stick, then tossed it over her shoulder into the bushes and buried her face in her hands.

"I guess we all make a carbon

footprint," I said. "There's no escaping it unless you live off the land like a hermit and eat dust." I imagined myself living in the wilderness with porcupines and wolverines.

"Or like Bigfoot," said Sie. "Now those are big footprints."

"Cut, cut, cut!" hollered Verna. She eyed Sie suspiciously. "What exactly do you know about Bigfoot, little girl?"

Sie leaned back and her eyes widened.

"Um, well, nothing really," Sie stammered.

Just then Howler walked up to Verna and whispered in her ear. A slow, wicked grin spread across her face.

"Buzz, Mr. Timberlake, could we have a moment please?" Verna sneered. The three put their heads together while Howler sniffed the air like Hunter on a scent. Then Woody stepped out and looked at us.

"Youse kits ain't seen or heard nothing...unusual, has ya?" asked Woody, looking worried.

"I heard loud growling last night," Martin said, his brown eyes bulging.

"That was T's stomach," said Sie.

"I heard scratching," said Marley, "but the cabin has a squirrel sneaking around. Probably living in the chimney."

Verna stepped in, arms crossed and toe tapping impatiently.

"Are you *sure* you didn't hear or see anything unusual?" she said, her eyes narrowed to slits. "Howler here is certain he can smell a Bigfoot around this camp."

"Snotcake Cornball here has big smelly feet," snorted Ivy, pointing at me. "They run in her family."

"Well, there was that loud sound we heard last night," I said, "when we were outside, running around."

"It went—Yooo-OOP!" Vi screeched. Everyone stood still. Talking hushed, my heart beat faster. I had to agree, that was what I heard, too. Here I had thought the noise was Ivy attacking Vi.

"Yer sure it weren't a toad or ki-yoot?" asked Woody.

"Yeee-OOOP!" Viola screeched again. The noise rolled out from deep within her short, squat body, sounding like a garbage truck backing into a train. I looked to see if glass had burst out of the cabin windows.

"Is *that* what a toad says?" she said quietly.

"And last night, laying in my bunk, I could have sworn I saw a bear outside my window," I said. "It never moved all night. I looked this morning but think it was just a stump."

"Verna!" Howler called from the side of the bunkhouse. "Take a look at this! Near this window."

Among the ferns near my cabin window there was a huge footprint, longer than my forearm.

Holy creeps! Had Bigfoot peered in my window in the middle of the night?

"You holding out on us, Timberlake?" asked Verna, now annoyed and no longer bored. "You know we're going to have to comb these woods now."

Woody shook his head no and bit his lip. Funny, but I don't think this is what Woody wanted to hear.

"Well dese kits have a hike to git to right now. So let's get dem outta here an' wrap dis up, eh?" said Woody, ushering us to the Firewood van. The *Critter Country* film team went into evidence-gathering mode with plaster and measuring tapes while the camera rolled.

"Mrs. Hills is going to show us the cabin she is staying in for the Porkies' Artist-In-Residence program. And show us around a bit," said Marley, trying to sound calm and keep her hands from shaking on the steering wheel.

FOREST STORIES

"I was hoping we'd get to stay," I moaned. "Things were just starting to get interesting. Holy creeps, I don't know if I should be scared or excited."

"I don't know if I should be skeptical," said Sie, rubbing her chin. T scooted closer to her mom.

"Come on guys," said Mrs. Hills, "It was probably an owl. I heard one just last night. Barred owls can sound like a bunch of monkeys squalling."

"Do owls have big, flat feet?" asked Martin, his wide eyes peeking out under his dreads.

"Tracks can appear larger in the mud, especially when the maker of them slides around," said Marley, who looked paler than usual. "Besides, the experts are handling this. More than likely it was a prank." I felt slightly disappointed.

"Anyway, Sasquatch is just one kind of forest story," she said, trying to change the subject. "There are different kinds of forest stories. We'll have the trees tell us their tales today."

"Trees don't talk," Ivy crowed from the back.

"Not in words, but in other ways," Mrs. Hills said with a twinkle in her eye. "We should all listen to trees. They have a lot to say."

We arrived at a parking area near a trailhead. The path climbed a tall, treed hill overlooking a gurgling creek.

"Now *this* is wilderness," Mrs. Hills said, stretching and spreading her arms wide.

"Where's the cabin?" asked Sie, looking around.

"We have to climb the hill," Mrs. Hills said, pulling out a large jug of water and shouldering a backpack. "It's about a quarter mile, back in the woods. We have to hike water and supplies in." Marley pulled on her own backpack with our lunches and handed Sie and I jugs of water.

"Wait—you mean we have to *carry* all this up hill a quarter mile?" I asked, looking at the filled water jugs. "These things are kinda heavy!"

Mrs. Hills patted my shoulder. "Being in the wilderness means no running water, no electricity, no corner grocery store. We have to provide everything we need to survive up here ourselves, gang."

We trudged along behind Mrs. Hills. But as we walked I forgot about the heavy water jugs—this place was like walking into a cathedral of trees. Everything was green, top to bottom. I could hardly see the sky. Sunlight filtered through the leaves to shine on ferns growing on the forest floor. The only sounds were the leaves in the wind and birdsong—and Martin, wheezing up the hill behind me.

"It's like a fairy forest here," said T.

"If it wasn't so scary…" said Martin, glancing over his shoulder every few steps. The forest was striped with shadow and scattered patches of light.

Finally we could see the cabin peeking out from behind a hill.

"This is it kids," Mrs. Hills announced. "My home for the next week." We set our packs and water jugs down on the long porch. In front of the log cabin wearing a long skirt, wide straw hat and tennis shoes, she looked comfortable out here in the wilderness.

She unlocked the heavy door and took us inside. "The only running water is when I jog up the hill with it," she joked.

There was no electricity, but there were oil lamps and a wood stove for heat. There was log-framed furniture, and a patchwork quilt-covered bed made the small bedroom under the loft look cozy and warm. Mrs. Hills' paintings of the forest lined the loft railing like party decorations. Her paint tubes and sticks were strewn across a large wooden table, and a coffee mug balanced atop sketchbooks and notes. Large windows looked out into the forest.

"Where's the bathroom?" Ivy blurted, taking a swig of water from her bottle. "This camper's gotta go." So Misty showed us the "facilities", an outhouse next to the cabin.

Behind the cabin ran a creek where Mrs. Hills gathered her bath water. There was a washtub leaning against the outside wall.

"Dirty dish water has to be carried away from the cabin so it won't draw in bears," said Mrs. Hills, gathering up art supplies.

"Bears!" Martin gasped, plastering himself against the wall. "What else is out here?"

"Well, the other day I saw a wolf," Mrs. Hills said. "Then there are fishers, who hunt porcupines, and lynx, who hunt rabbits." Martin began to hyperventilate.

"We're all together, Martin," Sie said, trying to calm him down. "Nothing is going to get us when we're in a group."

"The cabin and the critters are super cool, but the best part here are the trees," Mrs. Hills said, spinning about. "Trees! So many big, beautiful trees. And quiet. Lots of quiet!"

"This is awesome times ten. It's so primitive," I said. "I want to live in the wild." Out here, Mrs. Hills' carbon footprint was probably tiny.

"Are you kidding Shortstuff? Hah! Gimme my six foot flat-screen TV, air conditioning and heated toilet seat," said Ivy, sneering and popping her gum.

We followed Mrs. Hills and Marley down a trail into the woods. Marley showed us a cool nature clue, a small dusty bowl in the trail.

"This is a roughed grouse's dust bath," she explained. "Birds use dust to control parasites. The forest is filled with clues about who lives here."

"So that we don't forget these things we should walk softly and carry a big sketch pad," Mrs. Hills said, winking. "We need to remember to feel, smell, listen to and touch."

"The ground here feels like a sponge," I said, as we wandered over the soft forest floor. I wiggled my toes in my moccasins.

"It's the duff that covers the forest floor," said Marley "That's what the accumulation of needles and plant matter on the ground over the years is called. It's what makes the ground soft and holds moisture."

"The forest has different stories, or layers, of life, from the top to the bottom," she said pointing up. "The canopy is way at the top, and just below that is the understory and then the forest floor."

"Like layers of a cake," said T, rubbing her growling gut.

"Each level has life specific to that layer. Earthworms don't live up in the canopy layer."

"Trees are OK I guess," snorted Ivy, "There's big money in trees. Just think of the all the money you could make from them. You know—homes, furniture, toothpicks. There's a lot of *moolah* to be had here." She looked each lacy hemlock up and down.

"Trees contain everything needed for survival. Shelter, food and even water," Marley continued, ignoring Ivy and flipping the pages on her clipboard.

"Yeah, like our "pine-bark spaghetti", said T. "Speaking of spaghetti, is lunch soon?"

"As a matter of fact, yes," Marley replied. "Today we're having the forest floor for lunch." I knew our meals were organic but we were hungry and this was ridiculous.

"Forest Floor Pita Pocket," she said, laughing. "The pita is like the forest floor, holding the leaves, nuts and seeds that fall—spinach, celery, broccoli sprouts, grapes, walnuts and sunflower seeds. Everything that waits in the soil to grow."

After lunch Marley had us look at the ground where we sat, pointing out different things on the forest floor, like mosses, dead leaves, sticks, insects and fungus. Ferns, flowers and baby trees reached up from the duff.

"Did you know that the ferns of Early Michigan were once the size of trees over one hundred feet tall?" Marley quipped. "They were taller than many of the trees in this forest." I imagined dinosaurs tromping through the woods and insects the size of hawks buzzing overhead.

"Going up from the forest floor you reach the understory,

72

FOREST STORIES

canopy

understory

shrub layer

forest floor

COLOR the canopy BLUE-GREEN, the understory GREEN, and the forest floor YELLOW GREEN.

where shrubs and young trees compete for sunlight," Marley said, plucking a leaf from a nearby tree. Mrs. Hills helped us fold maple leaf cups for us to drink our water out of while Marley told us about leaves gathering sun and keeping roots cool and moist.

"And trees are homes for animals," said T, pointing at a squirrel running way up over our heads in the highway of branches. Martin ducked.

"They make good places for creepy things to hide in," he whimpered. "Like bats and bugs. I know trees are good, but there's so many and they're so tall it makes me dizzy. We only have one tree in our yard back home," Martin said.

"The tops of the mature trees is called the canopy," Marley explained. "This is where the leaves gather the sunlight and make food for the tree, which is stored in the roots, way back down in the forest floor."

"Out here there are yellow birch and sugar maple—they're deciduous—trees that lose their leaves," said Mrs. Hills, inhaling the spicy air. "And then there are the conifers—the cone-bearing trees, like hemlock, balsam fir, spruce and pine."

"And trees make oxygen," Marley added. "Trees filter the air and take in our carbon dioxide and give us oxygen."

"I like how trees have faces on them," I pointed out. "The lichens look like fuzzy freckles. And birches have eyes." They did kinda stare like Vi, but were more friendly.

"Ah," said Misty, "*In the thick woods so secret and enclosed you may seem alone but you are not, for there are always eyes watching you,*" she said. "That is a poem on trees. One of my favorites, by

Thalassa Cruso," she smiled.

"And now let's split up into our teams—" Marley began, but Mrs. Hills interrupted.

"Instead of two teams, why don't we all be just one art team—like a forest—all working together?"

Marley looked down at her clipboard of tree data, handouts and activities. Mrs. Hills was messing up her game. "Um, OK, Mrs. Hills, that sounds great," she shrugged.

"Let's go on a drawing adventure. Wherever you are is what you draw. Be a luna moth dancing on wide mint-green wings," said Mrs. Hills, spreading her arms. "Float and go wherever you please."

"Someone's been out in the woods a bit too long," Ivy choked and snickered, making a face.

Mrs. Hills pulled large sheets of brown paper and pastels out of her bag and handed them to us. We rolled our sheets and followed her into the forest. I felt like an explorer with primitive tools, drawing what we discovered.

We came to a place where some trees had fallen and were covered with fungus. An old yellowed birch in front of me looked like it had an owl face peeking out of it. Misty cried, "Stop, drop and draw." I collapsed onto the duff and drew the owl-faced trunk. A woodpecker drummed in the distance then flew to a tree not far from us. Black and crow-sized with a red head, it circled the tree cackling at us. The base of the tree was sprinkled with wood chips.

Sitting there under the tall trees, I remembered Gram telling me to listen to them. I wasn't sure what she meant so I sat quietly, trying to hear what they were saying. Then I noticed, off to my right in a patch of sunlight, three sticks lying in the shape of a tree or arrow.

Then Ivy broke the silence.

"All trees are brown and green," she groaned, falling on her back. But the trees in Misty's drawing were purple, gray, yellow, green and red. I liked her idea better. When I looked again I saw the colors she saw.

We went back down to the cabin on the trail along the Union River. Crystal water ran over mossy fallen trees and around craggy, rocky bends.

Back at the cabin Mrs. Hills said, "I'm out here looking for that one special Porcupine Mountain Wilderness scene to paint, the one that says it all. I haven't found it yet, but I will keep looking. I'll know it when I see it," she sighed.

"Well, we should head back," Marley announced. "We have a big day tomorrow—Union Bay beach and then the Presque Isle River. Ten points for both teams today." We all cheered.

SEEKING WILD SECRETS

We got back to camp to find the office had been ransacked. The books on the shelves were in a jumble, papers were scattered across the floor, and the back door was open.

"I don't think a squirrel did this," said Sie, picking up an overturned chair."

"Someone was clearly looking for *something*," Marley said, checking her desk drawers. The rest of us went around the whole camp checking for missing things and cleaning up.

"Maybe it was porcupines," said Viola, her eyes gleaming.

"Stop it, no!" Martin looked ill. "They shoot quills filled with poison! I'm too young to die!"

"The quills aren't poisonous and they certainly don't shoot them." Sie said, shaking her head. "Where do you get this stuff?"

"Nothing seems to be taken in here," T reported from the bunkroom. Martin ran in and hugged his cell phone and video game to his chest.

I pulled my bag down off my bunk and checked. My new, old backpack and its contents were secure and safe. No one touched my fossil collection, or my books on Michigan Indian's myths and legends. But I could not find my folding walking stick anywhere. Plus there were leaves and dirt on my bunk. I was sure Viola was up to her old tricks again.

I pulled Sie aside. "Vi stole my new hiking stick. Look at

her. Where was she when everyone was helping to clean up? She just sits there acting all weird." Vi sat on her bunk staring into space.

"You don't know that she did it," said Sie "How can you prove it?"

"Wait—whose side are you on?" I glared at Sie. Sie glared back. I was boiling and my freckles fried.

"All I'm saying is don't do anything stupid, Holly, check your facts first." Sie got down an old book on Weather Clues and turned her back.

I kept a close watch on Vi at dinner that night. She was not getting away with this. That hiking stick was special. Like Gram, I was going to hand my stick down someday to my own red-haired granddaughter. Now it was gone. I was keeping my eye on her.

After dinner, Marley announced that she didn't want to keep us cooped up when there was a pretty evening to sit around a campfire. We decided if there was anything dangerous going on, someone would have told Marley or left a note.

So she made popcorn and we gathered outside around the Clan Council fire and watched moths and bats flit about. A screech owl whistled and Marley whistled back. The owls actually came closer to us.

"They're out eating caterpillars and bugs," she told us.

Then we heard a tree frog and found it clinging to the cabin wall near the light, waiting to catch moths.

"Pretty cool," I said, "we're like animal trackers." Then T called us over to where a spider was working on its web in the silvery moonshine.

"Some spiders eat their webs in the morning," Marley said as we watched another spider wrap a trapped bug in silk, saving it for later.

Talking about spider webs had given me an idea. Before bed, while the others brushed their teeth, I snuck into the office and found a ball of rainbow colored yarn that looked like a scoop of superman ice cream. I would use it to set up a trap to catch Vi if she tried to raid my bunk. I would keep my flashlight handy to catch her in the act.

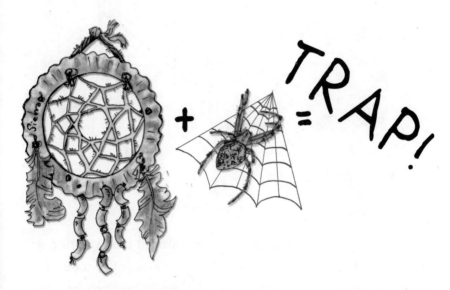

I set my trap right after lights out. I strung the yarn from the ceiling and every corner of my bunk. My own life-sized spider web/bad dream/culprit catcher. I tried to wait but I drifted off to sleep.

Scratching sounds woke me. At first I thought it was Sie sniffing but then it became more of a high-pitched squeak. I held my breath and waited for the next sound. I felt like something was watching me.

Just then what sounded like a claw scratched down the window next to me. It tapped and scratched again. With my heart pounding, I felt for my flashlight. Then something hit my bunk and landed on me.

"*Squee!*" the thing cried as it scurried over me.

"Yargh!" I hit my light. The thing bounced like water on a hot skillet across my bunk and then leapt across the room. I swung my arms wildly, getting tangled up in my own trap. Sie hopped down and ran over to see what the matter was while T went to turn on the lights. By the time the lights came on, Sie was also tangled in my web.

"Holly H. Wild," Sie snarled. Her glasses were snatched from her face and dangling like a fly in my yarn catcher. Incredibly, Martin was still asleep. Then Marley was standing in the doorway in her robe, arms crossed, her foot tapping the floor—fast.

"What...is...going...ON IN HERE?!?" she demanded. The flying critter that had bounced off my bunk was now on Martin's bed, crawling toward his face.

"*Stop it!*" I shrieked, and pointed.

"WHAT?!?" Marley leaped, her yellow robe flailing.

"That!" I pointed again. Marley looked over as Martin woke up. The critter bounced away from him and climbed up the bunk in a heartbeat. Marley ran to Martin's bunk but the creature flew from there to Viola and Ivy's bunk. Marley started to chase it but it flew straight toward her and landed on her head. She screamed bloody murder. The big-eyed creature  sat for a moment, caught its tiny breath then saw the open door and made for it.

"Flying squirrel," Marley panted. "Nothing to worry about. And Holly Wild, what is that contraption you have there?" Sie was un-weaving herself and her glasses from my multicolored polyester web.

"A spider web trap to catch Vi," I said. "She's been in my bunk leaving things and taking things." Vi glared at me.

Marley sighed deeply. "Vi, is this true?"

Vi didn't respond, but sat staring wide-eyed at me, her mouth slightly open.

"I'm talking to you, Vi!" Marley said. "Why are you staring at Holly?"

"I'm not staring at Holly," she replied quietly, and poked a pudgy finger in the air. "I'm staring at the person in the window behind her."

I tried to leap from my bunk but got tangled in my spider

web trap again. Marley walked shakily over to the window with Martin, Sie and T plastered to her. There was no face, but scratched on the dirty windowpane outside were letters.

"I can read backwards," said T. "it says 'PBJ'!"

"Peanut Butter and Jelly," I said. "I remember peanut butter and jelly. Seems so long ago."

"Now I'm hungry again," whispered T.

"Teams GEEK and SPORK, this PBJ is one pretty bad joke." Marley was really angry. She pulled the ratty curtain across the window, ripping it as she pulled. "First it was vampires and now this! I deviated from my clipboard and made you popcorn and then you do this. Ten points from both of your teams."

"But we didn't…" Sie said, shooting me an icy look.

"Sleep," she ordered, then marched out the door. We all looked at each other.

"How can we sleep after all that?" T asked. "Someone or something is still out there."

Viola rolled over in her bunk. Ivy was snoring by the time Martin hung up his blanket curtain with the dreamcatcher attached. I still didn't trust Vi.

DAY 4 (WEDNESDAY)

BIG WATER, BIG RIVER

The next morning Marley's whistle had us up and out of bed early. Breakfast was quiet. Marley, still clearly upset from the night before, announced the weather, bag lunch menu and that it was beach and water play day.

"Marley never even mentioned the events of last night," T said quietly. "She must still think we had something to do with the window message."

"I think we should get Dad, Aunt Kitty and Woody up here."

"Holly, I have a secret to tell you," T said, looking to see if anyone was near. "I found an old journal in the library when I was cleaning the other day. It was stuck inside a forestry book on timbering techniques. Anyway, I think you need to look at it. I had it under my mattress so Ivy and Vi wouldn't find it. I think someone was looking for it yesterday. Team Wild needs to go underground with this." My eyes felt like they were popping out of my skull.

Sie sidled over to me when the others went to wash their breakfast bowls.

"I thought you were Team SPORK," I squinted as my freckles eyed them suspiciously.

"It wasn't my choice. I didn't pick the teams," T whispered.

"Besides, I will always be a GeEK and part of Team Wild, silly."
My freckles got all warm and embarrassed-feeling.

"You may not be on our team, but look, Martin needs you,"
said Sie. "You're good for him. Can you imagine if he was
on a team with Miss Grim Reaper and Miss Poison Ivy?" I
shuddered at the thought.

T looked around then slipped me the mysterious book
under the table, got up and rinsed her bowl and casually walked
outside with Sie.

Its plain brown cover had a coffee-stained cloth binding.
A rusted star-shaped button with a string wrapped around
it kept the book's secrets enclosed. On the front was an old
photo of a boy with a gun. It looked like someone's diary or
scrapbook. A Yooper artifact! My heart leapt. Then I noticed a
tiny, fragile corner of a yellowed article sticking out. I slipped
it out and read the headline: *"Orphan, Woodrow Timberlake, Age
4, Loses Mother."* Holy creeps! Cousin Woody! I had to hide
this. I needed time to go through it properly, preferably with a
flashlight late at night.

I gently tucked it under my shirt and went into the

bunkhouse. Outside Marley blew her whistle. The teams were lining up with towels and gear and lunches for the day.

"Holly Wild, your team is waiting!" called Marley. "Five more points go to SPORK if you are not here pronto."

I slipped the journal into my new-old backpack and strapped it on. That way I could keep it close.

"I had to go to the bathroom again," I said as I walked up to the van. "I'm not feeling so great." I grabbed my belly and winked at T. Marley rolled her eyes.

"Our first stop is Gitche Gumee," Marley said.

"Bless you," Ivy snorted. T and Sie chortled.

"Gitche Gumee, as in the Big Sea Water, Lake Superior," said Marley, hands on her hips. "Home of the great horned, underwater beast."

"But that's a legend, right?!" yelled Martin.

"Yes, Martin," replied Marley a little wearily, as we piled into the Camp Firewood van.

We pulled up to the Union Bay Campground. I strained my neck looking out the window.

"Whatcha looking for Holly?" asked Martin, his eyes ever-scanning for danger.

"I'm looking for my Dad and the Beast."

"Is the Beast your mom?" he asked. Everyone snickered. Even Viola lifted a corner of her mouth ever so slightly.

"No!" I blurted, my freckles getting suddenly defensive. "It's our new–old RV,"

"Is that what you call that moldy antique?" shouted Ivy, fake-gagging with her finger. We drove past the Death Star with its hi-tech gadgets, satellite dishes and expando rooms gleaming in the morning sun.

"Teams," called Marley, pointing out the window. "There's

the big lake." Now this was the Superior of legend that I had heard of. Steel gray waves crashed against the rocky shore in a frothy splash.

We got out and went down to the water. There was no sand on this "beach". Reddish-brown slabs of rock stretched down the shoreline. Waves breaking over them left small pools in the cracks and crevices.

"Guess we're not swimming in this!" I said, eyeing the cold waves. We followed Marley along the slippery shore. Boulders and cobbles dotted the beach like Gitche Gumme itself chewed them up.

"Slate like a plate. Easy to break," Marley said about the rocks. We took turns dropping a few and breaking them. "Some

 of the sandstone has stripes, some have bubbly marks, and some have marks from wave action. Its another kind of rock found here in the Porkies."

"Wow, this big rock over here is cool," shouted Martin. "It's like a treasure chest of other rocks with red, yellow and black in it."

"That's a giant conglomerate," Marley explained, looking at a boulder the size of a cow. "It's clay with other rocks mixed in, mostly jasper and...." As Marley talked I wandered over to a polished log on the shore as long as a stretch limo.

"Wow! Look at this!" I yelled into the wind. "This could be the leg bone of a giant underwater panther." Sie snapped a picture of it.

Right then I spotted Aunt Kitty and Hunter making their way along the rocks.

"Hey!" I yelled, waving. "Aunt Kitty!" I was glad to see them both.

"Hi kids," she smiled. "How's camp life?" I wanted to say 'take me with you please', but I knew I had to persist and persevere.

"It's good, it's ok," I smiled a weird tight grin. "How's your bat tracking going?"

"Oh…um, good!" she said, a little unconvincingly. "We've got our eyes to the sky! Well, I'm here to relieve Marley for a moment while she speaks with Woody. I'll be taking you eco-challengers on a wildflower walk." I never thought I'd be so happy to hear those words.

"How can flowers grow in rocks?" snorked Ivy. "That's like so stupid."

"No, dear. That's survival," said Aunt Kitty. "Flowers have learned how to adapt and get what they need from where they grow. Bloom where you are sown," she said, her eyes twinkling. "They not only survive—but thrive." We looked at a delicate blooming blue harebell sticking out from a rock crevice next to where someone had made a little rock pile. There were other piles on the, some large, some small, like stacks of presents left on the shore. Some were decorated with black-tipped gull feathers, wilted flowers and shiny red berries.

"Those are rose hips," explained Aunt Kitty, pointing out the red berry. "That's the seed of the wild rose. I'll tell you the story while you make your own rock pile, which is called a *cairn*. People think if they build them the cairns will watch over the water and protect it. Think of it as a thank you note to the lake."

We all combed the shore for tiny treasures, found items and sticks to construct our own cairn. While I searched the shore I came across a symbol someone had built with three pieces of driftwood laid on the ground to make an arrow shape. Funny, that's the same thing I saw in the woods yesterday.

An icy gray wave reached up and plucked a cairn built too close to the water. This Lake Superior was cold, strong and as primitive looking as the rock, and held secrets like panther bones. Then Aunt Kitty gathered us on the sun-warmed slate and began her story.

THE ALMOST MOUNTAINS
HOLD SECRETS

"Long ago the wild roses lived everywhere. There were so many bright pink flowers that no one paid attention on the day they cried, "Help us! We are being eaten by rabbits!" *There seemed to be plenty of the pink flowers so no one listened to their cries.*

No one noticed—not the bear, the bee,

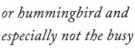

or hummingbird and especially not the busy human beings. That is, until the humans noticed that the bears were thinner that year. Until the bears noticed that there was less honey. And the bee and hummingbird noticed that there were fewer flowers to drink from. Then all the peoples noticed that the roses were gone!

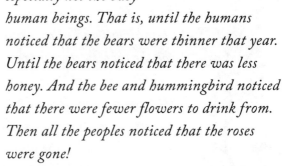

So naturally, the humans blamed the bear, who blamed the bee and the hummingbird. And the next summer there were no roses to

be found anywhere. Bee and hummingbird hungered. Bear raged. Humans complained. A

meeting was called and Hummingbird was sent out to look for the roses.

Hummingbird spent months looking for a single rose. Finally it found one tiny, sick

plant hiding on the side of a mountain, much like the mountains behind you. Hummingbird carried the pale, dying plant back to the people to be cured. "Who did this to you?" they demanded. "The rabbits—they ate us," replied the rose.

Bear roared in rage, "Let us eat the rabbits!" Lynx, wolf and bear each grabbed a rabbit by the ears and they punched the rabbits in the nose, which is why all rabbit have split noses and long, stretched ears today. And then when that did not satisfy the animals and it looked like a serious situation for the rabbits, the tiny rose coughed and uttered "STOP! It is not their fault. Had you cared and watched over us, if you had just noticed and listened to us, this would not have happened. It's partly your fault," she said as pale as a moth wing. "Leave the rabbits be." So after that day, all wild roses grew thorns to protect themselves from being eaten and are still pale pink."

"Gee," said Sie, pushing up her glasses. Viola sat and stared at the rock. Martin squirmed. and fidgeted

"Poor rabbits," said T, topping her cairn with an orange-red rose hip.

"So what you're saying is we shouldn't eat roses, right," asked Ivy. "Am I right, did I guess it? Don't eat 'em all cuz next time they might grow big and have poison pinchers and kill us and stuff, right?"

"No, Ivy dear," said Aunt Kitty, straightening a pin on her vest. "No, not at all. Not even close, dear."

"Uh. Don't send out stupid hummingbirds to do an eagle's job?" Ivy squinted. "It has to do with eating roses right? Thorns?" Poor Aunt Kitty checked her watch and slowly shook her head no. The story seemed to be losing its meaning with each passing second as Ivy yammered on.

"I know," I said raising my hand. "We need to be careful with everything, not to take too much. You can take, but you can't make something new—if it's all gone."

"Yeah! Don't eat too much rose flower salad," Ivy chimed in. "I knew it!"

"Just stop," Sie snapped at Ivy. "It's about survival. Loss of wilderness and habitat affects all animals big and small."

As Viola stared at her feet, Martin waggled his hand around in the air.

"Oh, a question!" said Aunt Kitty, clapping her hands. Martin looked up at his raised hand.

"Um no, I'm trying to get a cell signal." Martin waved his phone this way and that. "Are we going hiking now? I can't get a signal here. I figure up on the mountain I can get a signal. I didn't text my mom this morning."

"Why look, here comes Marley!" said Aunt Kitty, relieved.

"You're ready to rumble through the mountain wilderness."

As we drove over to the Presque Isle River, Marley filled us in on the day's challenge.

"This will be a good hike to prep you for our mountain hike tomorrow, when we will put all of our skills to the test," Marley said, gripping her clipboard.

"I hate pop survival quizzes," moaned Ivy. "This camping adventure is too much like school."

"We will hike down to a suspension bridge overlooking the cascades," Marley continued, ignoring Ivy, "then we will head up river to see three waterfalls. We'll stop for lunch where the South Boundary Road crosses the river, then head back up the other side."

We tumbled out of the van in the parking lot near the mouth of the Presque Isle River. "Team GEEK and Team SPORK," announced Marley, checking the map flapping on her clipboard. "Today we will get to see water in action and have a sort of scavenger hunt for our next challenge." Oh, good, I liked scavenger hunts.

"I want you to look for three things—something that lives in the water, something that has been changed by the water, and something that uses the water."

We walked down a long stairway to a bridge high above the rushing river. The rocky riverbed below looked like it had been made by a giant ice cream scoop. Water poured into each bowl and swirled before running downstream.

"These look like footprints made by Babe the Blue Ox as it clomped all over the river!" T exclaimed.

I looked again at the swirling river. "Hey, wait a minute—did the water make these bowls?" I asked Marley.

Marley smiled and nodded. "Very good, Holly, it did indeed.

92

Water rushing through this valley for thousands of years helped carve the riverbed. The rock is called Nonesuch shale, and as the water swirls down the riverbed, pebbles get caught up in the eddies and chips away at the rock, creating these potholes. Five points for Team GEEK for identifying something the water has changed!"

COLOR Paul Bunyan and Babe the Blue Ox in the river!

Martin slapped me on the back. We were so gonna rock this challenge! Marley had us take out our field note journal and sketch the cascades.

We crossed the river to the far bank. Tall hemlocks rose above us. Their tangled roots made designs and pictures in the trail, which were toe catchers. I wished I had my hiking stick with me because I tripped three times.

The trail widened out and became flat and we could walk out onto rock along the river. There were pools of standing water here and there, and plants grew in the cracks and crevasses. The shale was layered like a sandstone cake.

"Hey, look!" Martin called, "there's tiny pickles floating in this water." He pointed to a small pool shaded by a rock ledge.

"Those are tadpoles and other little wiggly guys," I said, poking my finger at them, trying to tickle their bellies.

"Very good, Team GEEK!" beamed Marley. "You've identified something that lives in the water. Five more points for your team." I exchanged a fist bump with Martin.

"So can we drink this stuff?" Ivy scooped up a handful.

"NO!" said Marley loudly. "Everybody freeze!"

"Remember your dad, Ivy?" asked Sie. "Did you not learn anything back in Empire?" Ivy dropped the water like it was poison. Sie told the teams about giardia and not to drink directly from a lake or river, that it needs to be filtered first or it gives you diarrhea.

The tadpoles' tadpool was a cool home. Marley pointed out ferns, lichens and spleenworts—which sounds gross but were really pretty—growing out of cracks in the stone, which shaded the pools. I wished I was tiny and could swim with them in their tadpool.

We could see Lake Superior at the end of a short channel. Marley told us about Pressie, the local legendary underwater monster of Lake Superior, and that some people had seen it at the mouth of the river. She said that one guy even got a snapshot of it. I wondered if Pressie was the underwater panther of Native American myth.

We continued down the trail to the first waterfall.

"This is Manabezho Falls—" Marley began, but I cut her off.

"Manabezho! I know him! Well, not personally," I said, hoping for extra credit. "I remember the stories of Manabezho from Beaver Island." Marley went on, reading from her clipboard, apparently unimpressed.

"Manabezho Falls are one of the tallest in the park, with a drop of 22 feet."

We walked for what seemed like forever. It was hot and

the sun beat down on my bare head. Martin was wheezing and my feet hurt. Moccasins on rock were not great when you were used to hiking boots. There were two more falls along the way, Manido and Nawadaha, both smaller than Manabezho. I was too tired to be excited about them. We finally reached the bridge and Marley found us a shady spot to have lunch.

"OK, Eco-challengers, we've gone just over one mile," she said as she passed out our lunches—Log Roller Wraps stuffed with avocado egg salad in a tortilla with granola on the side. We sprawled in the shade eating our inside out mossy logs.

The hike back was a drag. We'd seen it all before, walking down the opposite bank. Maybe it would have been fun if it hadn't been so hot. It was not too long before Martin and I lagged behind.

Finally Martin sat on a rock and I stopped to let him catch his breath. Marley must not have noticed that we dragged like an anchor as she jetted on. Then Viola came back down the trail.

"You guys coming?" Vi whined. "Marley said stay to the left and go up the hill for a shortcut."

"Yeah, OK," I called. We got up and moved on. A shortcut sounded good right now. My Log Roller wrap was doing some major log rolling in my belly. We finally came across a thin path that veered off to the left.

"Vi said to take this shortcut," I said, so we left the main trail and began to climb. We climbed higher and higher as the path grew more narrow and overgrown. Below us the water rushed and roared. Martin gasped and stopped, then gasped and stopped again.

"This is really narrow," he said between breaths. "Are you sure this is the path?"

"Yeah," I said, but I was having doubts about Viola sending us this way. I started feeling like the roses in the story, like everyone had forgotten about us! Then suddenly the path stopped. A fallen cedar blocked our way.

"Oh boy," I said, looking down, "it's really, really steep. Don't look down, Martin." Now I felt like the rose hanging on to the edge of the mountain by its teeth. The river made me dizzy looking at it rushing by. There was nothing to do but go down the way we came. But we would have to back down—meaning hike backwards down a steep, steep hill above a fast, mighty, cold river.

"Martin," I said, "it looks like we have to go back." He started breathing too fast.

"I knew—we should—have stayed on the trail," he wheezed. "We shouldn't have listened to her. Now we're lost—we're gonna die!" Tiny rocks rolled past his feet.

"Hold on cowboy," I said, gripping my moccasin toes into the trail. "First, slow your breathing down. OK?" He calmed himself and nodded, shaking.

"Number one, we backtrack," I said in my best brave voice. "Number two, we're not lost. Number three, no one is going to die." If I can wrassle a caiman and dance with bear cubs I can do this, I thought. Just stay calm is all. And upright.

"M–maybe if I—get a cell signal— I can call for h–help—w–whoa—WHOA!" he said as he reached for his phone, nearly tumbling backwards.

"Martin! NO!" I yelped. My heart nearly stopped. Martin caught himself and shifted his weight. He teetered a bit, rolling more stones and sliding. His knees started shaking.

"I feel dizzy. I feel sick," he whimpered. "I-I didn't call my mom this morning."

"Martin, slow down," I said. "Listen to me. It's simple. We backtrack. No phone. Remember the trees. Listen to the trees." I was trying to think of anything to make him calm down. Then

I remembered that trees scared him and here we were with giant trees looking down on us. He shook more.

"If I fall in, Pressie will get me," he wheezed. He tried to reach for his dangling inhaler.

"Stop!" I commanded him. "You're not going to fall in, because I say so. You're a GeEK now Martin, one of us. Geo-Explorer Kids never give up." Then he peeked down at the roaring water, still frozen but shaking less.

"I can't do it," he said. "It's too far to go backwards, I just wanna keep going up. We can do it. Just climb over the log."

"If we did we'd be doing our own log rolling on the river. Who knows where the trail ends or who made it—what if there's no path on the other side?"

"You mean like an animal made it? Like a porcupine or cougar?" he whined, his panic ramping up again.

"Hey, you like games," I said, trying to change the subject. "You know the game Mother May I?" He nodded. "Well this is Martin may I.

"Martin may I take one step backwards?" I said looking behind me briefly. He chuckled nervously. He took a deep breath, his shoulders tensed. He moved one foot. Then the other.

"Yes, you may," he said letting out his breath, and we each took one step. It worked!

"Martin may I take two baby steps backward?" I asked. He nodded and we stepped. My plan was working. We took two more baby steps and paused and then two more and two more. The water got louder as we got closer.

I kept talking to keep him focused and calm.

FISHER

"Hey, Martin, did you ever think about your name?" he shook his head slowly. "Martin Fisher, those are weasel names. Maybe if you think like a weasel you can climb like a weasel. Weasels are hunters. Martens hunt squirrels. And fishers hunt porcupines." He tried to laugh.

"Good, they can't poison us with their quills when I'm around," he said. "Holly, may I take three baby steps in case a porcupine comes along?"

"Yes, you may." This time he stepped more confidently. "I'm feeling hungry now with all this hunting weasel talk. Hey, maybe that's why I like porcupine meatballs. My mom makes them with spaghetti." He moved a little bit further this time without asking.

"Yeah," I laughed. I had no idea what he was talking about. "I'll have to get her recipe when we get out of here."

"Sure," he said, one more step down, "I can email you her recipe. They're easy. I help roll them—" His foot slipped a bit but he caught himself. I could hardly breathe myself, hearing the water roar below us. "In fact, maybe you can come over and I will make them for you. Rice is the key ingredient. The rice are the poky quills—only not poisonous." He took two more big steps backwards.

"Glad to hear it," I said. I glanced over my shoulder to check our progress.

"I could eat a whole army of porcupine meatballs," he said as we stopped to catch our breath. At this point we were finally able to turn around and hike back down to the main trail.

"You did it!" I howled, smiling with relief.

"I am Martin Fisher the Third," he yelled to the water when we reached the bottom. "I am Weasel Boy!"

The two of us whooped and howled and gave each other high fives before collapsing onto the ground laughing. He never used his inhaler once.

"Man, you really had me worried," I said.

"*I* had me worried," Martin replied.

"We're home free, now!" he said. We looked up and there stood an open-mouthed and angry-looking Marley.

"Oops," I said.

"I heard all the yelling," she said, fists clenched. Now she was the one shaking. "Whatever gave you two the idea to stray off the path? You could have slipped and rolled into the river. I am taking away all your points for the day—plus five more for YOU TWO not listening to orders...UGH!" she stomped her foot.

"But Viola...!" I said. "She told us to take the shortcut!"

"Save it. We have to catch the others," Marley said, marching double-time down the trail. Martin and I stumbled after her. Sure enough, Vi and the SPORKS had taken the right path and were waiting for us. And Vi was eating the last of T's gorp with extra M&Ms.

SECRETS IN DA NIGHT

We stopped at the campground on the way back to camp. Woody had pie irons cooking in the fire. Cherry bubbles oozed out and sizzled in the flames. Holy creeps, they smelled super-tasty times ten.

"Hey kits, got time fer d-zert?" asked Woody. I wanted to stay in this camp with their cherry pies and even smelly old Hunter. He grinned at me like he knew I was thinking about him. Then he reached over and ate a whole package of hot dog buns. I thought about the newspaper article from the journal.

"Cousin Woody, I have a question," I said. "What happened to your mom?" Forks dropped. Spoons clanged. Hunter whined and crawled under the camp picnic table knocking over ceramic mugs. Dad cried "Holly!"

"W-what's dat you say?" Woody cleared his throat, looking very uncomfortable.

"I mean," I stammered, "I miss my mom, and I'm sure you miss your mom. So, um, what happened to her?" I asked, stumbling over the words and now wishing I'd never asked.

"I do miss'er, dat's fer sure," he sniffed, pulling out his snotrag and blasting into it. "I miss her every day. It was–it was da storm dat took her."

"Dis is da anniversary of her...being missing...officially. Sixty years ago today. Dey never found hide nor hair of her even

101

doe dey looked and looked."

"Was it lightning, or a flood?"

"Geez, Holly," Sie growled a whisper to me.

Woody held his huge paw up. "No, da kit has a right ta know. My mom was a good woman. Da best. She taught me all she knew. Here one minute, gone da next. It was da tornady of 1953 dat took her away from me. She was in da kitchen, cooking up a storm, so to speak, fer da camp men-folk when da sky got all black an' swirly. I taught she burned da biscuits or sumpin but naw, it was da dark sky and da meanest twister dis side of Saginaw, ya."

He took time to blow his nose again. "Dat twister come barrelin' down on us like a steam engine huffin' and puffin', eatin' everyting in its path. Next ting I know I'm an orphan. Just a pup I was." Woody honked his nose. Aunt Kitty patted his shoulder. I gulped. I felt bad for both him and his mom.

"My mom, my breakfast, my house, gone. Good ting I was under da table or I'd be gone too. Dat twister ravaged da trees. Dey'd been tru fire an' flood but never a twister. Twisters don't give up. She takes and takes and twists," he said, twisting a newspaper into a tight roll. He tossed it into the flames and it flared. "Don't know much about her. I just remember what she taught me. Always she said, 'Kit! You stay under da table when I cook!' Good woman. Fine woman."

"Geez, that's awful Woody, I'm really sorry," I said. Everything was quiet until Ivy broke the silence like a shattered glass bottle upon the rocky slate.

"So does that mean your mother is extinct?" Ivy said, chomping on a hotdog bun that Hunter had missed.

"Uh, yeah, I guess," Woody said, getting up. "Excuse me kits, I need to go do sumpin'." He honked his nose again as he entered his RV.

"Ivy," said Sie, her head in her hands. "That was so rude."

"What? Extinct is the opposite of survival which is the struggle to stay alive or something Marley said, and she obviously didn't persist or persevere." Fine time for Ivy to actually learn and remember something.

"Well Sarah, Tina," Dad said, "I need to go talk to the big guy. Good night kiddo." He scruffled my head before he went inside the RV.

Aunt Kitty walked us to the van. Even Aunt Kitty had lost her fairy twinkle and seemed sad. "You look so much like her," she said, pinching my cheek and giving me a hug.

"Who?" I asked, but Marley shut the squeaky van door. Who? I mouthed at the window. Gram, my mom, who? I slumped back into the seat. Vi stared at me and Ivy belched. Ugh. Back to Camp NorthWood Misery.

When we got back to camp, I really wanted to look at the diary again. Maybe it would say more about Woody and his mom. And why would it have been hidden in the bookshelf?

Marley and the others whipped up vegetarian pizzas. Lumberjack Pizza she called it: Asparagus, green onion and broccoli on a pita "*saw blade*". I figured it couldn't be worse than what Aunt Kitty sometimes feeds us.

"Oh I get it—these aparisguts and broccolis are the trees on the Lumberjack Pizza!" Ivy blurted. "Pretty clever Miss M." She slapped a pencil-thin green onion onto the pizza. Marley smiled and blushed and made a check mark on her clipboard recipe. Ugh! For Ivy to shine made me ill.

Sie and T were designing their pizzas and arranging the veggies into patterns. Vi ate hers one item at a time from the tray without putting it together. Martin was asleep at the table, drooling on his pita.

Sie looked at T who winked at her, then knocked over a jar of tomato sauce. Marley jumped up and ran for paper towels. Sie pulled me through the bunkhouse door. At last, secret revealing time.

"We heard Ivy on her cell phone," she said, looking back into the kitchen. "She left a message for someone. I think it was in a secret code."

"No way!" My pulse raced, my freckles sparked.

"She said the porcupine walks at midnight. She said it left a message for all to see. Bring the beast to the nest."

"What the heck does that mean?" I scratched my head.

"T and I are on it." Sie watched for Marley. "We're working overtime on the clues. Meanwhile, you keep an eye on Vi. I think she is up to no good."

"I know," I said. "She nearly got us lost—or worse."

"But really," Sie said, sounding irritated, "you couldn't just listen to simple instructions and stay on the trail? What were you thinking? That was dangerous and cost you a lot of points, and you could have gotten hurt." She slid back into the kitchen as Marley finished mopping the spilled sauce.

I steamed like a pile of asparagus with extra cayenne and poblano peppers. I decided right then that I did not need any team. I was on my own. No Gram. No Dad. No Aunt Kitty. NO Team Wild. I needed no one. I am tired of trying. From now on I am solo amigo, lone wolf, a single Wild thorny rose among stones. Holly H. Wild now stands for Holly "Hardheart" Wild.

I was not looking forward to after dinner free time after the day I'd had. The teams were outside playing tag but I stayed in the bunkhouse. T ran in while I watched the others play.

"Why don't you play with us?" she asked. "It's fun. We're all playing. A first for Vi," she whispered.

"I'm tuckered. Heading to my bunk, topside, to get shuteye.

If you need me you know where to find me."

"Need you? What's wrong?" T scowled. "Why are you talking like a cowboy?"

"If yer not with me yer against me," I snarled. T looked confused and shrugged her shoulders. I climbed up to my bunk. Golden evening light filtered through the pines and danced across my sleeping bag.

I could hear them laughing outside. I pulled back the spider carcass-encrusted curtain to spy on them. Even Vi ran in her awkward flat-footed way. Ivy laughed and made jokes and T and Sie laughed at them. I turned away.

What to work on first? Go through the diary or decode Ivy's message? Ivy. Vi. Huh, never thought about that before, but Ivy was Vi backwards. I shivered. Vi was the total opposite of loud animated Ivy. Ivy was tall and gangly like daddy longlegs with a big head and pointy teeth. Vi was short, squat, with pale eyes.

Bring the beast to the nest. My mind was in puzzle mode now. I had to load pieces of information into my hard drive to fit them together. *The porcupine walks at midnight. Left a message for all to see.* I touched the letters scrawled on the window. PBJ. My stomach growled again. Outside the teams were snacking on organic, free-range watermelon.

Did Ivy know who left the message on the window? Was the "beast" connected to this Bigfoot thing? *Bring the beast to the nest.* What was the nest? The cabin? Did they plan on catching the "beast" in action and bring it here? What is the "beast" anyway? And what did this have to do with porcupines?

My puzzler was puzzled, so I decided to look at the diary instead. I slipped out of the bunkhouse without anyone noticing and crawled into my dilapidated shelter. Right inside the entrance I saw another arrow shape, like my tree symbol and the symbol I saw on the beach. It didn't look like it was just from sticks falling in—someone clearly placed it there.

Holy creeps times ten! Maybe Gram was right. The trees *were* saying something!

SECRET JOURNAL SECRET

My flashlight beam illuminated the pieces of mildewed, moth-eaten cloth scraps stapled inside the journal. *Baby's first blanket* was written under a piece of red striped wool. Other bits of fabric were also labeled—*First cooking apron; age 4; first school dress, age 8.* Woody wore a dress to school? OK, that was strangely confusing.

The journal smelled of maple syrup and pine sap—oddly familiar. Then there was the *Mining Journal* news clipping and another, from the *Ontonagon Herald*, dated June 30, 1953: Storm Takes Mother Leaves Young Boy Orphaned. So who was Woody's mother? I scanned the article. When it came to her name it was cut out!

There was a baby picture of him and the newspaper article photo of the orphaned Woody. Husky, tall and chubby-cheeked with freckles and a puff of mushroom hair, you could almost see a beard sprouting already. Holy creeps.

PBJ

Then I found a wrinkled photo with a scrap of cloth stuck to it with syrup. I moistened it with spit and peeled it off. A big, wild-eyed, wild-haired girl in a plaid wool shirt and dirty apron holding an enormous cast iron skillet looked out at me. She was bare-footed. I flipped it over and looked at the back of it.

A chill ran up my spine. The initials on the back read PBJ, like the letters on the window! PBJ, like peanut butter and jelly, my favorite sandwich in the whole world times ten. PBJ was also handwritten on a tiny corner of heavy tan paper sticking out below the dress swatch. I pulled it out.

A report card from 1932! "I showed this card to my parent" was written across the front. The PBJ that initialed that statement on the front of the card was none other than Nonesuch resident Pauline Bigge Junior. Pauline? Could this Pauline Bigge be my famed Yooper cousin Pauline Bunyan?

I'd seen Gram's old photo of her that was smudged and chewed up from mice. It had to be her. I was giddy with questions and no one to ask. I wondered why she was not a Bunyan but a Bigge. Yet another family mystery in the family tree. That tree was full of them, and it was about time to go picking! I opened her second grade report card carefully. I remembered my report card in second grade was not so hot.

Ciphering: B-

Timbering skills: A- Pauline knows how to tend and plant, needs encouragement on proper cutting techniques. Advise a timber tutor. Sharpens knives well.

Weaponry: B Pauline's target practice needs improvement. Shotgun care excellent. Throws knives and hatchets well.

Survival Skills: A+ Pauline skins and tans hides exceedingly well, needs work on firemaking.

Home Economics: C- Pauline burns eggs. Needs work on flapjacks.

Gymnastics: C- Pauline is clumsy and awkward. She runs like a three-legged moose.

Behavior: C- Gets along well with others if they are animals. Pauline is a loner, quiet unless angered.

Listens to Instruction: D Pauline, although a self-starter, refuses to take advice and exhibits headstrong tendencies.

It was eerie how both of our report cards were pretty much the same, except I didn't skin animals—yet. Mom won't let me use a knife. But the clumsy awkward thing was spot on with me and my dad. Uncanny. There were more photos of Pauline, one of her sitting with a shotgun across her lap, Age 5. Wow. At age 10, my age, she was as tall as Dad and had one bandaged foot poking out beneath her long dress. She looked like Woody, only without a beard.

I looked down at my growing feet. Maybe I was getting my growth spurt this summer like my brother Boy had last year. Then it hit me—I thought back to Pauline running like a three legged moose. Maybe she wasn't Pauline *Bunyan,* as in the legendary hero, but Pauline *Bunion,* a nickname about her sore foot! Gram had a bunion, until she had surgery. Bad feet run in the family.

I had to look closer since my flashlight was dimming and yellowing. There was an old black and white photo of the town Nonesuch, a weird name for a tiny town, and a map-like drawing of the town and mine from the 1880s. There was a real old photo of two men in front of a building, Bigge's General Store. Written in ink was "Gus and George, Bigge Brothers".

Gus and George
Bigge Brothers

Another yellowed photo showed a large, unsmiling woman who looked a lot like Woody, wearing a long dress with a tiny bird perched on her finger. "Honey 'Hawley' Halliwell" read the name on the back. This photo looked even older than the one of Pauline—could it be her mother? She had big, frizzy hair and freckles too.

It seemed that Pauline's whole family history was in this journal. I touched the initials on the report card, the same letters that were scratched on my window.

Only daylight would bring clarity and understanding—and breakfast. My belly was growling from missing dessert tonight. I wish I could tell my former Team about this discovery. My heart felt heavy under the egg-shaped moon. Eggs and PBJ.

I put the journal under my shirt and was getting ready to crawl out when I looked up to see Vi standing silently outside my shelter.

"What's that?" she asked, eyes narrowed, pointing at the symbol on the ground.

"Oh, um, that?" I stammered. "It's, uh, nothing, just some sticks that fell there." I smiled my best smile, trying to look casual. It never works.

"Mmmm hmmm," Vi replied. She stared at me for what seemed like forever then said, "Marley said to come in—NOW."

DAY 5 (THURSDAY)

A REALLY BIG SHOE

"Has anyone seen my phone?" squeaked Martin as we were waking up. I looked around and noticed Vi was gone.

"She probably took it," I said, pointing at her empty bunk.

"Holly, you're always blaming Vi for everything," Sie said, shooting me a look.

Out in the dining room T picked up a phone that was laying on the counter.

"Is this it Martin?" she asked. Martin rushed to grab it, relieved. "I take it that's a yes." Vi sat at the table, eating a bowl of granola, never looking up.

After breakfast we loaded our gear into the Camp Firewood van and drove back out to Lake of the Clouds.

"Been here, done that," Ivy whined as we pulled into the parking lot.

"Eco-challengers," Marley announced, ignoring Ivy, "for our next Wilderness Challenge, we'll be hiking the Big Carp River Trail along the Escarpment. We will be looking for food clues. Food is the next and last key to wilderness survival that we'll be talking about."

"Sounds like fun—not!" popped Ivy. Holding her gum in her

teeth she pulled it out of her mouth about a foot and wrapped it around her finger. "Is camp done yet?"

"That's it—I've had enough of your comments!" Marley said to Ivy. "I am taking five points from team SPORK for their blatant misconduct."

"But we didn't do anything wrong!" T and Sie complained. "Why should we get punished?"

"Because you're a team, and you get treated as a team," Marley said and marched off down the trail.

I couldn't help but smile—this would even things out some. Sie caught me smiling then turned and followed Marley up the trail walking fast.

"Team GEEK and Team SPORK, here is the heart of the Porkies," Marley said once we reached the Escarpment. "From up here you can see 35,000 acres of trees, old-growth forest that has never been cut. It's the last large stand of mixed hardwoods and of hemlock in Michigan. Some say it is the biggest and best tract of virgin northern hardwoods in North America." Ivy yawned and drooled. But I listened intently. It was like a voice— the voices of 35,000 acres of trees. Listen to us, they said.

"Talk about survival," Marley said, sweeping her arm wide, "these trees have persisted and persevered fires, storms and floods. It's all about survival."

"Trees take nutrients from the ground and use them to make leaves, nuts and berries," Marley continued. She pushed up her crooked glasses and juggled the clipboard and a food chain chart with yarn connecting plants to animals. "Food from the trees becomes food for turkeys, squirrels and deer, among others. Those animals become food for the predators—wolves, lynx and so on." The clipboard finally won in an explosion of papers and guidebooks. We all laughed.

"This is serious stuff! We need each other to survive. Like a team." Marley was beyond frustration. I folded my arms across my chest in obvious disagreement.

"Some animals don't," I said.

Marley looked frazzled. It had been a long week for her and us. "And Vi, where in Halley's Comet have you been?" she demanded, shaking.

"Following that bird," croaked Vi, coming up the trail behind us. She pointed out over the Escarpment.

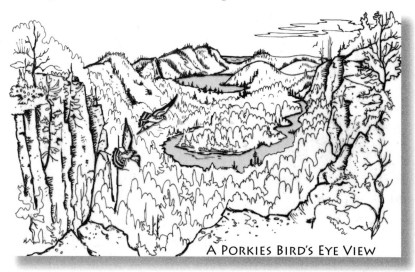

A PORKIES BIRD'S EYE VIEW

"That—that's a peregrine falcon!" Marley squealed. "They're endangered. You just saw an endangered species! That's not even on my clipboard!" she said, dropping her books and fumbling with binoculars.

"Maybe if you did less yakking from your clipboard you'd see more," snorted Ivy. She had a point. The rest of us nodded. Standing on the edge of the Escarpment Marley looked tiny and pale. Her face contorted and her nose reddened as she fought back tears.

"We'd have more fun," said Martin, scratching his leg. Marley's eyes watered and her lip quivered. She'd been a good sport with this crew. I felt bad for her.

"What if we make it a game instead of a challenge?" I suggested. "Ask the Naturalist. When we see something we'll yell "nature clue" and you can tell us all about it." Marley's eyes lit up.

"That's a great idea. We can make it a game," she squeaked.

"And we can just have fun and do it and not give points," Sie said, looking over at me. She flashed a tiny, quick bit of a smile.

"No points!" whooped Martin. "I'm Weasel Boy and I say let's have fun!" The others stared at Martin. "I stared death in the face and prevailed," he said, grinning.

We walked and pointed and Marley shot us names and naturey factoids.

"Nature clue!" yelled T, pointing at what looked like a dried out, white-tipped worm on the trail.

"That's grouse poop," said Marley, flipping through a book, "the same bird that made the dust bowl at the artist's cabin." She showed us a picture of a grouse.

"Boy, that bird really gets around!" Martin joked.

"Nature clue, times two!" I yelled and pointed at a pile of dried, white poop on a rock ledge. Sie took pictures while Marley opened the book.

"Wow, that sure looks like lynx scat!" exclaimed Marley, showing us the photos in the guidebook. "They are not very common, but this is certainly the right kind of habitat for them—dense forest with rocky areas. They eat primarily snowshoe hare. This scat is old and bleached by the sun, but will still hold clues." We poked the poop with a stick and found crunched up bits of bones.

"We need to tell Aunt Kitty about this!" I said excitedly. "They're tracking lynx."

"They're what?" Marley asked, but Ivy interrupted.

"Nature clue!" Ivy slurped, popping a juicy-looking berry into her mouth.

"Stop!" yelled Marley. "You should ask someone before you eat anything out in the wild, it could be poisonous!"

Ivy opened her mouth. "It's gone—see. Can I have more? That was good."

"You're lucky this time, Missy," Marley said as she went back into camp counselor mode. "That was a blueberry. This is blueberry season up here. Next time ask first." We each tried some. They were good, warm and sun-kissed sweet.

"Nature clue!" Martin said, pointing out his first. "It looks like a pie."

"Like a blueberry pie," joked Sie. Marley stiffened.

"No, that's a very fresh pile of bear poop," she gulped. We looked around. Funny, I never thought much about bears being up here.

"OK, it's time to head back!" Marley announced loudly. "We'll just keep moving—noisily, so that we don't surprise any bears along the trail. Bears love blueberries too."

"But...we haven't gone very far!" Vi protested. We all looked at her, stunned that she'd said so many words at once.

As we neared the trailhead and parking lot, I was looking at a nest T had pointed out when I nearly tripped and fell over three birch branches in the trail. The three branches were in the shape of an arrow, and pointed down the Big Carp River Trail, whre we had just been. My freckle flags went up and I looked around. This could not be a coincidence. Was someone sending me a message? Were we being followed? What if I turned the arrow around and made it point the other way?

Chapter 18

Nonesuch, Not Quite a Boomtown

While eating lunch back at camp, Marley announced we would be going to the old ghost town of Nonesuch. My freckles just about exploded.

"Wait, what?" I stammered, remembering the photo of Nonesuch from the old journal. "You mean, that place is *here*? In the Porkies?" Marley nodded.

"Nonesuch?" asked Ivy. "No such town? A town that never existed? Or it's extinct? Like Woody's mom?"

"Yes and no," Marley explained. "Nonesuch does not mean extinct, it means the greatest or most prominent. The Nonesuch Lode turned out to be the richest copper lode in the state. Nonesuch, the town, grew up around a mine on that lode, but that particular mine was never very productive, and only operated for about 60 years. The community survived for a while by farming and logging, even though the town and mine did not. But over three billion pounds of copper were extracted from a mine just three miles east of there."

Ivy's eyes had glazed over, but I ate up every word.

"Well, I hope we don't see any ghosts there," Martin said, and shivered.

I wasn't worried about ghosts. I was so excited I couldn't finish my lunch. I wrapped up my nuts in a napkin and shoved them in my bag. This was the home of my Wild roots, and I could hardly wait to see what was there. I was actually hoping we would see a ghost!

It was a clear, blue sky afternoon as we hiked down the open trail to Nonesuch. We saw lots of scats belonging to fox, birds and coyote. It was a regular pooping highway from animals crossing into and out of the woods. Then we stopped in a large clearing and Marley announced we were in "town". She pointed out apple trees and daisies that must have once grown in someone's garden.

Down near the river we saw what was left of an old copper processing building, roofless, its stone walls crumbling.

"This was the stamping mill," Marley explained, reading from her clipboard. "This is where they separated the copper from the rock. There was a water wheel in the river that powered the machinery. This is pretty much all that's left of the town."

It was hard to imagine there was once a town here. It looked

Nonesuch 1884

pretty much like an old farm field. But it was kind of neat to think that people once lived here, kids went to school, played ball, maybe even told ghost stories during long winter nights, never knowing they would be part of a ghost town themselves one day.

We made our way down to Nonesuch Falls and played and waded in the shallow river.

"Hey, cool, I found a walking stick." I yelled. It was tucked up against an overhanging stone ledge along the river, like someone had set it down for a moment and forgotten it.

"It looks like something's been chewing on it," said Sie, examining the tooth marks.

"I'll bet it was a beaver," I said. "It looks like the poking stick I found on Beaver Island."

"It's awfully big and heavy," T said, hefting it. "Seems too heavy to be a walking stick. It would tire me out." She handed it back.

"Whatever," I said, "It's my Wild artifact, and replaces the walking stick Vi stole from me." Sie rolled her eyes but she wasn't going to argue.

Marley handed out snacks. I was too excited to eat, so I put mine in my pack. We explored the area of the town a little more, finding more garden-type flowers and bricks scattered here and there. The sun was starting to dip towards the horizon.

"OK teams, time to start the hike back," Marley called.

I wasn't ready to leave yet. I hadn't had much time to explore and look for clues from my ancestors. Then I had an idea.

"Hey, Marley," I said, "can we come back and camp overnight here? It would be so sweet!"

Marley shook her head no and started down the trail.

"But wait!" I shouted, following behind her, dragging my new hiking stick. T was right, it was heavy. "You've been talking all week about survival. This place has everything we need—apples for food, water in the river, even an old building we could make camp in! So what do you say?"

Marley stopped and turned to face me. I gave her my best smile, but she shook her head again.

"You can't just camp anywhere you want," she said, "even though it's a wilderness area. There are campgrounds for that, and there isn't one here. Plus, we don't have the gear we'd need to camp in the backcountry."

"But—" I protested.

"But NO. It's just not safe." Marley turned and marched off down the trail, clutching her clipboard. T and Sie looked at me for a moment, then followed with Vi and Ivy.

"Fine!" I said. I stood in the middle of the trail holding my beaver-chewed walking stick. I looked at the stick, then at the trees around me. I decided then and there I was striking out on my own.

I had been waiting for my big camping adventure but it never happened. The bear cubs had put an end to our campout at Sleeping Bear Dunes, and now that I was in an actual wilderness I was stuck in a smelly, rodent-infested camp building. And now, so close to my Wild relatives, I decided to stay behind and fend for myself. I had water in my bottle, I had leftover lunch and snacks, and I could camp under the rock ledge along the river.

I turned to go back down the trail and nearly collided with Martin, who had been standing behind me the whole time.

"You're really planning something aren't you?" He sounded almost sad.

"It's secret," I mumbled.

"Not if you're telling me you have a secret," he said. "Besides, we're GeEKS."

"I am my own team. Team Hermit. It's been good knowing you," I said. "Go on back with the others. I'm heading out on my own."

"B-but," he mumbled. He gave me a sad puppy look.

"You better hurry. I'm fine. I'm a survivor." I said. "I have persisted and persevered like the trees and mountains."

"Aren't you—scared?" he asked, blinking at me. I didn't want to answer him or think about that.

"Pinky swear you'll keep quiet about this," I said. We did and then he lowered his head and trotted in a dance of bouncing dreads up the trail.

When he had turned the corner and was out of sight I felt a twinge of panic mixed with excitement. Maybe leaving the camp was not a good thing in a place where bears drop their business cards. But I couldn't turn back now—I'd look stupid. And scared. No, I had to go.

CALL ME HOLLY 'NONESUCH' WILD

I had all my worldly possessions with me as I walked on. My tin cup rattled. Cicadas buzzed. Grasshoppers leaped. Cottonwood leaves applauded my journey as they clapped in the slight breeze. I went back to Nonesuch the way we had come.

"I saw a kind of a cave by the river," I said out loud to myself. "That nice crawl space where I found the walking stick."

The space was damp and cool, more of an undercut in the rock than a cave. Leaves were pushed into the back of the space, and spider webs hung down and got tangled in my hair. I took my pack off and crawled in, and tried to sit down, but the roof wasn't quite high enough. I guess at least I could sleep here. I turned around to face the river and laid down, my pack as a hard, lumpy pillow.

"This is more like it." I lay in the cool shade watching the water gurgle over the rock.

Shelter. Water. Food. Freedom. Who knew that freedom could be so quiet! I swept up some grasses and leaves into a pile on the hard rock floor. Home—this was home now. A breeze caught my hair. My cave must have been shelter for an animal, because it smelled kind of like an unbathed Hunter after he rolled in deer poop and garbage. Then it dawned on me, what if that animal wanted to come back here to get out of the sun?

Holy creeps!

Then I heard a rustle. I looked for a weapon but all I had was my heavy walking stick and my serrated plastic fast food knife. But when I reached for the knife in my pocket I found it was broken, maybe snapped in half when I crawled in my shelter. Rats, times ten.

The leaves outside the cave rustled again and I held my breath, my heart pounding. Then a chickadee appeared at the cave opening. Whew! He looked me up and down then flew off.

I sat in the damp, smelly cave, cobwebs in my hair, listening to the river. Freedom. The sound of running water made me thirsty so I reached for my water bottle, which I discovered was half empty. Half full sounds better when you are in the wilderness alone. I guess I'd have to ration my supplies. But first I had to list what I did have with me: An orange from breakfast; some nuts from lunch; my afternoon snack; a broken plastic knife; moccasin laces; a bandana; my journal; Pauline's journal; my canoe pen; one clean pair of underwear; and a half full bottle of water. Hmmm.

I reviewed my survival skills. How did that go? Four minutes without air. Four hours—or was it days? without shelter. Or was that water? Shelter— everyone needs shelter. Bears need shelter. Bears sleep in caves. Bears smell bad. This cave smelled bad. Suddenly I couldn't breathe and sat up in a panic, banging my head on the low ceiling. I was starting to think that maybe this wasn't such a good idea.

I crawled out on all fours and dragged my bag out behind me. Think—where could I go? Trees. Gram said listen to the trees. My mind raced like a squirrel.

I realized that Marley never went over fire-making. Maybe that was tomorrow's challenge. Maybe she didn't want us kids playing with matches, being in a forest. It was getting chilly and I had no fire making stuff. What would I do about winter? Think like a squirrel! I could make clothes from garbage bags, stuffing hem with dead leaves and tree bark like a squirrel nest, although tree bark sounded scratchy and I didn't have a garbage bag with me.

I couldn't hunker down here for the night, the bear might come back. Then I heard what sounded like a moose bugle, or a huge rusty hinge squealing. My heart jumped into my throat as the rustle and squealing got closer. Then out of the cedar shadows stumbled…

"Martin!" I fell backwards against the riverbank.

"I'm a survivor too. I got rid of my inhaler," he said, beaming and wheezing.

"Why did you do a fool thing like that? What if you need it? I can't just whittle you one," I spit in the river, trying to look tough, but it mostly ended up on my chin. I wiped my mouth nonchalantly looking away.

"I know." He hung his head. "I guess I didn't think about that. I didn't want to go back to camp without you. We're a team. You shouldn't be alone out here."

"It's OK. There's stuff I didn't think about either." He flashed me a panicked look. "At least we're together." I shrugged. He was obviously relying on me for our survival. Gulp.

"You and me are Nonesuch residents now," I said. "We are rare and unlike others."

"Unrivaled! We're the greatest," he tossed back his dreads. "Weasel Boy and Wild Girl."

"First things first, we need to make a shelter," I said.

We gathered big sticks and branches and leaned them

against a tree, tipi-style, then covered it with ferns and leaves. Then we pushed a bunch of leaf litter inside. We made it just big enough for us to crawl into.

"How did you learn to build this fort-thing?" he asked. "We didn't go over this."

"If you remember, this is how I started ours that first day at camp. Anyway my Gram taught me. We would build them in the back yard at home."

"Brilliant! I like making forts. If you think of it like we came out here to build forts then it doesn't seem so scary," he said settling in. "I built a fort at home with sheets over dining room chairs. But this one is really warm and cozy."

"Yeah. First night without my Team." It was starting to get dark in the woods and I realized that I was about to spend a night in the wilderness. I swallowed hard.

"I thought I am part of your team." He looked hurt. Oops. He was right. Here I had told him he was a GeEK and all.

"I didn't mean it like that. You are. I meant without my... other friends."

"I wanna be like you and have lots of friends," he said.

"Well, you already have us. We'll be your friends. But that Vi is another story," I said, and whistled. "Scaring us by saying she is a vampire, throwing hornets into our shelter, tripping Ivy, trying to get us lost at Presque Isle, stealing my walking stick—"

"And taking my phone this morning!" Martin chimed in. "Why did she have to steal it? I would have let her use it if she'd asked."

"What do you think she's up to?" I asked. Martin shrugged. "Oh, and then today up on the Big Carp River Trail, she was lagging behind, remember? And on the way back, I found an arrow-shape on the trail, made out of birch branches, pointing in the direction we had gone." I drew it in the dirt.

"It keeps turning up," I said, scratching my head. I hope I didn't have fleas. "I first saw it at the artist cabin. Then I saw it again on the beach yesterday, and last night there was one inside the shelter I built at camp."

"I saw that one on the trail, too," he said, pointing at my drawing. "And I saw one like it back at the camp near your window the day the film crew was there," Martin said, eyes wide. "I thought it was just firewood someone had dropped and I picked it up. It's like someone is watching us."

"Oh," I said, my freckles quivering. "I thought it was Vi messing with me, but maybe someone *is* trying to communicate with me." Then I happened to glance down at his shirt. He was wearing a Camp Firewood T-shirt, with the campfire logo on the front. And that's when it hit me like a ton of logs.

"Holy CREEPS Martin, that's it!" I pointed at his shirt and leaped up, knocking half our shelter over. "That's the symbol I've been seeing! Where did you get that shirt?"

He looked down at his shirt, then his eyes widened.

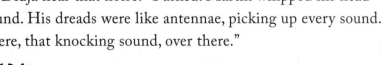

"I spilled blueberry juice on my shirt today after lunch so Marley gave me this one to wear. Do you th-think th-they're after me??" Martin squealed, beginning to panic.

"Who would be after you, Martin?" I asked.

As if in answer to my question, a loud knocking sound came from woods near the river.

"Didja hear that noise?" I asked. Martin whipped his head around. His dreads were like antennae, picking up every sound. "There, that knocking sound, over there."

"M-maybe it was a wo-woodpecker?" Martin said hopefully. "There's lots of them here."

I scanned the woods.

"Do you think Marley left?" he asked. "I mean, someone had to tell her we weren't in the van. They had to notice."

"I don't know if they care. Ivy could care less, Vi hates me—" Then we both heard a crashing sound—closer to us than the tree knocking.

"Something *is* out there," he whispered. "Probably a porcupine with quills aimed at us." From the shadows came a loud "yooooo-WHOOOP!" It seemed to bounce in front and behind. We didn't know where to go.

"Do porcupines make that sound?" Martin asked, shaking.

"I dunno, the only one I ever met grunted like it had to poop."

That made Martin laugh out loud, and he clapped a hand over his mouth. The crash came closer, sliding down a hillside. I thought about the berry-eating bear and its smelly cave.

"Don't run, just don't run!" I said. Martin shivered. "If you run, you trigger predator instinct."

"You've learned a lot here at camp," he whispered.

"I really had learned a lot before I got here, from my Gram and Aunt Kitty," I whispered back. "Thing is, I don't know which way the trail is." I fumbled in my pack for my flashlight, but it was tucked safely under my pillow back at camp. Maybe Marley was right and this wasn't safe without the right gear.

Just then we heard heavy breathing directly behind us, and something big crashed through the brush.

"It's the Y-Yooper!" Martin whispered, then fainted dead away. Just before he collapsed I saw the biggest feet ever appear from the biggest body ever out of the forest shadows. I looked up. Way up. Up into the creature's face.

Chapter 20

NONESUCH BEAST AT NONESUCH MINE!

"Gruuunhh!" the beast gurgled hoarsely as it reached down and picked us up by our collars and pulled us along. Its silvery fur glowed in the dim light. Its legs were like raggedy tree trunks on big feet.

"Where are we going?" I yelped. The dark beast heaved us limping and grunting through the brush and dropped us in the middle of the trail, then disappeared without breaking stride.

"Mom, I don't wanna go to school today," mumbled Martin, in a heap in the middle of the trail. In the distance I heard howling, yelling and shouting. Martin started breathing fast and looked at me. Then the baying closed in. Hunter?

"Don't say anything whatever you do," I pleaded. "It's our secret, OK? At least wait until we've had a chance to investigate. I don't want the film crew to find out about this." He nodded.

Within moments we were blinded by flashlight beams.

"Where the Heckle and Jeckle have you two been?" Marley yelled, running to us. She was furious.

Dad and Woody bounced behind her with Hunter baying to wake the dead and straining on his leash. He was sniffing big time, first me then Martin, and then he turned his big nose towards the woods.

"Dad! What are *you* doing here?" I asked.

"What are *you* doing here, young lady?" Dad looked worried and REALLY mad. "What were you thinking, Holly?"

"Aw, it's in the kit's blood Wooff," said Woody. "She can't help hittin' da trail."

"Yeah, wanderlust," I said, hoping to get off the hook again. "Just ask Gram."

"Holly, you both could have gotten hurt or worse." Marley

picked up something in the dim light. "And it would be best to take better care of your gear." It was my walking stick!

"Martin, are you OK? Do you need medication?" Marley asked. He was trying to slow his breathing while Marley fished out a new inhaler from her pocket and gave him a sip of water.

When he finally caught his breath he filled his lungs and bellowed:

"BIGFOOOOOOT!"

Hunter tried to bolt after the beast while Dad tried to bolt back to the parking lot. Woody and Marley took one look at each other then scrambled. They stood back-to-back, flashlights piercing the growing shadows as the sun set.

"Where? WHERE?" Marley yelped, fixing her glasses.

"It dragged us to the trail it knew we were out here it must have been watching us IT'S OUT THERE!" Martin shrieked.

"We should go—NOW." Dad said. He looked pretty pale. "Really, we need to go NOW."

Just then a blinding light blasted across the two-track trail, illuminating us and the surrounding woods. Gravel ground under tires as a large SUV skidded to a halt mere feet away. Doors slammed and there stood Verna and Vi.

"Good job, sweetie," Verna said, her lip curling in a reptilian grin. Vi grinned back. "Unlike your cousin Ivy, you do the Buckthorn family proud."

Cousin? Ivy? Buckthorns? Holy creeps!

"We've been following you for days. But one of you brats changed the marker Vi made for us at the Escarpment and sent us on a wild Bigfoot chase down the wrong trail, but we've got it now!"

"Pronto, people! Cameras! Action!" Verna clapped her hands. I locked eyes with Vi, my freckles blazing. Then Vi looked away and climbed back in the SUV.

I was stunned. There in the blazing light stood Verna, in her safari gear, with the *Critter Country* film crew scrambling around behind her in a haze of dust. Buzz appeared with a spotlight, dressed in black commando gear, and shone it out into the woods. Laser stood behind him, holding something at his side. Howler pushed past Dad and let out an ear-splitting "Yooo—OOOP!"

"I got eyes!" hollered Buzz, and we all looked to see two tiny lights shining back through the brush.

"Get out there girl!" Verna ordered, and shoved me into the woods. "It's been following you this whole time, see if you can lure it out!"

"Hey! That's my daughter!" Dad exclaimed and jumped in between us.

"Well, then we'll use Martin!" Verna said, and reached for Martin's arm. "That's why we brought him here in the first place. We need these kids tas bait o draw the Bigfoot out where we can film it!"

"You're not touching Martin," said Marley, grabbing Martin's other arm. A tug of war was about to ensue when Buzz gave out a yelp.

"It's coming closer! The eyes are coming towards us! It's working, it's working!"

I could see the red glow of eyes bobbing up and down as the creature came slowly closer. Then Laser raised what looked like a shotgun with a huge scope on top up to his shoulder and took aim at the beast. Dad and I gasped.

"Dad, they're hunting it! Make him stop!" I cried.

But before Dad could move a muscle Woody lunged at Laser,

knocking him to the ground and snatching the rifle-mounted gizmo away from him.

"Hey, that's my best camera!" moaned Laser as he clutched his shoulder.

"What?" stammered Woody, who looked down at the contraption in his hands. Before he could react, Howler snatched it back.

"We have it now!" Verna hissed as Howler readied the

- - -

camera. We all stood back and held our breath as the eyes moved even closer.

Suddenly Buzz sprinted forward, dropping the spotlight. He let out a war cry, rushing the beast, his headlamp blazing. But moments later he let out a cry of pain and his headlamp went out. We all gasped.

Verna picked up the spotlight and shone it towards the moans coming from the thick brush. There in the beam was

Buzz, bent and yowling, covered in porcupine quills. A porcupine sitting in the tree above him had swatted Buzz with its tail. We watched as it climbed down the tree and waddled off into the night.

"Cut! Cut!" yelled Verna, holding her face in her hand. Howler helped Buzz back to the trail, and gave a long. slow, quiet whistle.

"Better luck next time, boss," he said, and lead Buzz back to the SUV.

We stood in stunned silence while the *Critter Country* crew piled into their vehicle and backed down the two-track. Dad took a few steps forward, then yelled into the night, "What kind of parents are you?"

RETURN TO H.Q.

It was pretty quiet all the way back to Camp Firewood. Martin and I were in big trouble times ten, though I'm sure whatever happened to us when we got back to camp would not be half as bad as what Bigfoot could have done.

Aunt Kitty, who had been holding down the fort, met us at the door. Woody, my dad, and Aunt Kitty exchanged looks as Marley sat down. Team SPORK eyed Martin and me. Ivy popped her gum loudly.

"You kits stay here," Woody said, clearing his throat and looking super serious. "We adults got some talkin' ta do." They gathered in Marley's office and shut the door behind them. There was chattering and arguing.

"Here's your dinner, guys." T brought over grub. "Aunt Kitty whipped up some Lost-and-Found pasties for you. Leftovers from the week stuffed into a tortilla wrap."

"Gee, thanks," I said, eyeing the gloopy mess oozing out both ends. Martin shoveled his in as fast as he could. For the first time I was glad to be in camp, and glad that I had not become camp fare for a beast myself. I bit into the black bean, rice, avocado and walnut "pasty."

"So, what happened? Did you fall or get lost?" Sie asked.

"I ran away. Hit the trail. Struck out on my own," I said, licking my fingers. "I wanted to camp out."

"You too?" Sie asked Martin.

"We're a team," he said, spraying crumbs in Sie's general direction. "Buddy system."

"I'm so tired of this team thing," T blurted. "You guys could've gotten hurt—or worse."

"It wasn't my idea for it to be a team. My plan to head off into the wilderness was foiled by him and the hairy beast." Oops, times ten. Martin looked at me and I shrugged.

"Beast?" croaked Ivy. Sie and T looked wide-eyed at me too.

"Yeah, what do you know about a beast?" I asked, turning to Ivy.

"What?" she fidgeted. "I don't know nothing about a beast. What are you guys talking about?"

"You know. As in *bring the beast to the nest*," I said squinting my freckles at her.

"H-how did you know about that, Snorkelberry?" she glared back, crossing her arms, shifting from one foot to the other.

"I have Wild powers," I said, my freckles flashing. I caught Sie rolling her eyes at me.

"*Now* what have you and your creepy family done?" I demanded, getting in Ivy's face. "What sinister plan are you cooking up this time?"

"Hey, hey, take it easy Snozzleberry," she said, backing up. "I really don't know nothing! All I know is Verna promised me Zombie Mayhem III and ice cream if I told her when I heard anything unusual."

Just then then the office door flung open.

"Kits, we gots to talk to youse guys," Woody said, ducking under the doorframe, followed by Marley, Aunt Kitty and Dad. This didn't look good. From the looks on their faces my punishment would be far worse than I imagined.

"We got a confession to make." They all looked at each other then at us. There was a lot of sighing and shifting from one foot to the other going on. There was a BIG secret times ten about to be revealed!

"You see…." Dad fidgeted and coughed, Woody scratched his beard. "Um, we here are the B.E.A.S.T." My mouth dropped open. They were the beast?!

"B.E.A.S.T.," said Aunt Kitty, "Actually stands for the Bigfoot Emergency Action Search Team."

"So it was real. It did happen." I said. "There *is* a Bigfoot up here in the U.P. and Martin and I met it?" There was a collective gasp from Team SPORK.

"We here, all of us," Woody gestured to the group of gathered adults, "have met it at one time or another."

"I guess that makes Martin and me part of B.E.A.S.T. now!" I grinned at Martin. He smiled weakly.

"You're absolutely right, Sugarpie," said Dad. "You've had your own experience." T and Sie stared at us. Pretty cool. It was even cooler that Martin and I weren't in trouble—much.

"Bigfoot touched my head while napping," said Woody, sniffing, "outside my cabin years ago."

"And I'll never forget smelling and hearing Bigfoot," said Aunt Kitty, "I was a college student out

doing bat cave research for my paper while visiting Woody. You don't forget that smell— dirty feet, mixed with vinegar and garlic." She shuddered, wrinkling her nose. Martin and I nodded in agreement.

Bigfoot's stench did make my eyes water.

"I saw Bigfoot when I was a kid visiting Cousin Woody's cabin not far from here," Dad explained. "My brothers Buck and  Jake and I were out in the woods playing. Suddenly they ran back to the cabin and locked me out." Dad shuddered. "A storm came up so I went into a shed. Lots of thunder and lightning, lots of wind. Then I looked up and saw a face in the window staring at me—about 7 feet high." Dad was wringing his hands. "I screamed and it took off. I never wanted to go back out in the woods after that day."

"Martin and I not only smelled, saw and heard Bigfoot," I said, glancing over at T and Sie, "but it dragged us to the trail. And we lived to tell the tale." Team SPORK's mouths dropped in unison.

I described the events of the evening, from me leaving the group and Martin showing up to our encounter with the beast and the arrival of the film crew.

"Film crew?" Sie asked. "Where did they come from?"

"I dunno," I replied. "Ask Vi. She was there too."

"Speaking of creepy Vi, where is she?" Ivy blurted.

"As if you don't know," I glared at Ivy. She made a face.

"I'm not psychotic ya know, Stinkweed. She bolted when we got back here from that No-such-place." Ivy sneered.

"That's true," interjected Aunt Kitty. "Young Miss Viola ran out to her parents' SUV in the driveway. I was glad to be rid of her. She's a strange child."

"That's an undergarment!" snorted Ivy. "I'm her cousin, I

know." She rolled her eyes and made a whirling cuckoo motion around her wobbly head. I can't imagine being part of the Buckthorn family. Holy creeps.

"But where is she now?" I asked.

"She must be with her parents," Marley said. "She didn't come back with us."

"We found out that Vi has been spying on you kids and reporting back to her parents," Dad said. "They wanted to use you guys as bait to lure Bigfoot in so they could film it. I doubt Vi will be back."

"But from da looks of it, da film crew will be busy in da clinic fer awhile. Mr. Buzz Vetch got swatted by a porky tail—in da face." Aunt Kitty gasped then twittered behind her hand.

"So what was the message from Ivy about bringing the beast to the nest and the porky walking at midnight?" I asked.

"Ivy must have overheard me tell Woody to bring the Beast, or the RV, here to pull down the other hornet nest on the chimney," Marley said. "We had to get up high enough to reach it. And a porcupine had been in camp chewing on the doorframe at night. We needed to trap and relocate it."

"Oh," I said. "And what about this, 'it left a message for all to see'?"

"Oh, that," said Marley. "Woody saw some bear scat behind the kitchen door and I had to remove it before you kids saw it." T and Sie's eyes grew like melons. Then everyone burst out laughing. Now my freckles were popping in embarrassment.

"What about the track and 'PBJ' written on the window—explain that!" Martin demanded. "And what about the Bigfoot b–beast?"

"The track and window message still baffles us B.E.A.S.T.s," said Aunt Kitty, looking over at Woody. "But I believe this Bigfoot is friendly."

"We need to git back out first ting in da morn an' track it," said Woody, wiping his brow.

I stayed up late with T and Sie, filling in the details about the night's adventure. Martin was sound asleep in his bunk. I don't know if Ivy slept or not, but I was not about to share any information with her now that I knew she had been secretly working with Verna.

I described the beast but Sie was not buying that it was Bigfoot, insisting it was probably a bear that was going to eat us until Hunter scared it away.

"But bears don't drag people by their collars," I said to Sie. "Bears use their mouths. This thing grabbed us both with its hands like we were two bags of groceries." Sie shrugged.

"I just think Bigfoot is not real is all," she said. "There must be some scientific explanation." T was quiet.

"Well, I believe it was Bigfoot," I said, and smiled. "And Woody, Dad and Aunt Kitty must believe, too, because they're here looking for it."

When we finally turned in I couldn't sleep. I decided to get the journal out and look at the pictures of Nonesuch and Pauline again. But panic set in as I rummaged through my pack. The journal was gone!

DAY 6 (FRIDAY)

ARTIST-WAS-IN-RESIDENCE

After our Friday Breakfast, a Squirrel Surprise Bowl of nuts, eggs and blueberries, we heard Woody pull up outside. Dad, Aunt Kitty, Hunter and Woody were ready for their B.E.A.S.T.ly tracking.

"What are we gonna do while they go look for it, Marley?" T asked. I could tell Marley wanted to go.

"Free day," blurted Martin, waving his video game in the air.

"Go with?" I suggested. Marley leaned against the window watching them load gear.

"No chance," she said spinning around. "Too many of us could spoil track evidence. And you get into too much trouble."

"Why don't we visit my mom?" suggested Sie. "Hang out in the forest for a day."

"Sure, that works for me," said Marley, nibbling on leftover stale Paprika-basil Popcorn. She turned away from the window. "I gotta do your camp report cards anyway."

"Report cards?" I moaned and crumpled on the table.

"We all know whose team is tops," Ivy howled. "You cry-baby losers had no chance with me and my girls here." She threw her arms around T and Sie. They cringed.

Just then the door flung open. Woody pulled Marley aside.

Not again! Marley looked worried, it was serious. She looked at us then nodded.

"Team," Marley said. "Looks like we are all going tracking after all. Get your gear ready!"

"Bigfoot can wait," said Ivy, squishing a grape between her pointy teeth, kicking back in her chair, feet on the table.

"It's not about Bigfoot," said Woody. "It's about moms. Moms always come first," he sniffed. "Da artist lady. She's lost in da woods."

"Mom?!" the girls choked and dropped their forks. They turned pale, then jumped up.

"Looks like she been gone since early yesterday. Kitty took Mrs. Hills her special baked Lavender Lemon Surprise Pie yesterday morn. When she got dere she found a note on da table saying she was out finding her painting. Whatever dat means. Dose paintings just can't get up and walk on dere own donchaknow." He honked his nose in his red hanky. "Last night Kitty tossed and turned and wanted to tell Misty you kids were OK, so she went back first ting in da mornin' but she was still gone. Guessin' she was out all night."

Woody teared up. He might be a big, hairy, hardy tracker guy, but he was really a squishy, gentle giant, especially when it came to moms. "At least yer mom left a note." He blasted his honker again.

The twins leapt from the table and we rushed to the bunkhouse to get our gear, then sprinted to the RV. Marley dragged Ivy like Bigfoot dragged us. I shoved Martin in mid-inhaler squirt.

"We're goin' to track her before we track da Bigfoots, donchaknow," Woody assured the twins. "I'm sure she's OK. We got Hunter here. He's a good sniffer, dat dog. "

Dad wheeled the Beast out of the parking lot, laying a patch of skid marks on the asphalt. He ground gravel as we turned onto the dirt road leading up to the Artist-In-Residence cabin, leaving pots, pans and our brains rattling as the old girl roared and charged ahead.

"Her special painting," said T, twirling her hair bobs. "She's must be looking for that one special scene. I hope she's OK."

"I'll bet she didn't have camping or overnight gear with her," Sie said, chewing her nails. "If I told her once I've told her a hundred times to always be prepared for the weather. Moms!"

Dad slammed to a halt at the head of the trail, leaving cabinet doors swinging, hangers clattering out of the closet. We tumbled out the door. Hunter howled and dragged Woody over the mist-covered Little Union River bridge and up the steep gravel hill.

Hunter led us up the hill to the quiet little wooden cabin. Misty had her easel set up on the porch and the rocking chair faced out to the fire pit. A pair of binoculars sat on the railing. Had she seen something mysterious and strange? Light crept through cracks in the forest canopy.

A pail of water sat on the porch near a towel. Aunt Kitty and Woody went in to the cabin to get a sweater for Hunter to sniff and get Mrs. Hill's scent. He bayed and waggled his tail, then bolted for a bag of Doritos on the table.

"Mom?" called Sie and T. It was eerily quiet in the cabin. Her art supplies were laid out on the table. Her bed was neatly made, a shawl hung over the rocking chair, and a tea bag sat next to Aunt Kitty's uneaten pie.

"Misty!" hollered Dad out on the porch.

"OK fellow B.E.A.S.T.'s, let's split up. Kitty, me an yer hound will take Misty's kits." "Wolff, Marley, you take dat girl and Holly," Woody said, pointing at Ivy.

"I got my survival gear on," Ivy bragged. "Latest technology. Expensive stuff." I sighed.

"What about me?" Martin squeaked. Woody scruffed his beard.

"Oh, sorry 'bout dat, didn't see ya. You team up wit Holly dere lil feller. Youse guys got lotsa eyes and we'll follow da dog's nose. Right now he is pointing right up dat trail." Martin beamed at me.

Once Hunter got a whiff of Misty, he dragged Woody back down the hill towards the parking area and the bridge over the Union River. We hustled to keep up. But Hunter seemed to lose the scent once we got to the river.

"We'll follow the river to the right," said Dad. "You guys go left. Meet back here at two o'clock. If you find her give three blasts on a whistle." He held up the day-glo orange whistle around his neck.

We walked along the banks of the river, searching for tracks or other clues to Mrs. Hills' whereabouts, calling her name as we went.

We must have walked for half an hour when Martin yelled "Nature clue!"

"We're not out here to discover wildlife, dimbulb, we're out here looking for a dippy artist," groaned Ivy. Martin scowled and pointed.

"Here." On the rock sat a paintbrush and a carbon stick. Dad picked them up and dropped them in my backpack then he scratched his head.

"We can't be sure if she may have dropped those before yesterday. But, let's go just a little further."

"Misty!" Marley called. No answer.

"Nature clue!" Martin called again.

"Martin," Marley whined, "no wildlife clues, please."

Martin pointed to an eight-point deer antler lying on the pebbly riverbed. "I hope a wolf didn't do that," he said.

"No," said Marley, "bucks shed their antlers in late winter. It has marks where rodents chewed on it—it's probably been here since at least last winter."

"What's that over there," Ivy asked. She pointed to the other side of the river at what looked like human tracks.

"Someone crossed the shallow part of the creek," said Dad. "Fresh tracks are down by the water."

"Maybe she got hot or thirsty," Martin said.

"But why would you cross the creek if you were just thirsty," I said. "Maybe she saw something on the other side." I pointed at track marks like a slide on the hill. "She sure has large feet," I noticed.

"Probably from sliding in the mud," said Marley.

"Let's go," Dad said. "It's worth a look-see. Watch for slippery rocks." Just as he said it he did a river dance, sliding, balancing and splashing before he landed on the other side on his butt. The rest of us crossed the creek with less fanfare.

"The tracks go up that hill," said Marley.

"Woody said there were wolves up there." Dad shivered.

145

"Hope she didn't get swallowed by one—you know, Lil Red Riding Hood style," said Ivy.

"You guys aren't helping. Let's just hope that's not the case," said Marley. "Hey, look another clue—a paint rag."

"Or her bloody tattered clothing," said Ivy.

"There's paint on it," said Marley, giving Ivy the evil eye. "And if she bleeds in green and purple then she has more trouble than wolves. This must belong to Misty." We trooped up the hill climbing over rocks and boulders.

Martin wheezed. "Let's take a break gang," Dad said. "Pull up a rock, son." He patted Martin on the back.

"How about a drink and a granola bar?" Marley handed us each a blueberry bar.

"Too bad that dog's not here," said Marley. Dad checked his watch again.

"I almost forgot. We said we'd meet up at two—we really should be heading back. But we are really on to something," he said. He was not so good at being in the deep woods OR making decisions. He scratched his head and arms

"I'll go up and you stay here," he said to Marley. "You can't get lost staying by the river."

"I have my hiking stick, Dad, I can I go with you—it has a compass." He thought about it.

"Sure," he said. Then he turned to Ivy who was poking moss with a sharp stick. "What you got in that pack, Irma?"

"Huh? Oh, first aid, searchlight, GPS, emergency blanket, stuff," said Ivy, peeling the moss back.

"Wow, all that! Can we borrow it to go look for Misty?" asked Dad.

"No can do Mr. Wildguy," said Ivy. "It cost my pop a cool $1,475 on sale. He'd kill me if you and Snotblast took off with it. Where it goes, I go."

"Fine, you can come along then, Ida," Dad said, sounding tired and desperate.

"*Daaaad!*" I whined. He shrugged. Maybe he brought her along in case wolves showed up 'cause then he could use "Ida" as bait.

"If Misty is hurt she'll need the first aid. You two have been together all week—what's another 10 minutes?" he grinned.

Glaring at me, Ivy pulled out the extended visor of her cap and unfurled her neck protector cloth in the back of her hat. I slid my bandana around my head and tightened it down. Ivy snapped a headset over her hat and plugged it into her way finding device. I whipped out my hiking stick and shook it. It snapped into place in one piece. She bent over and pushed a button on her shoes and they inflated to mountain climbing mode. I retied my moccasins.

"Let's go," I said to Dad. He sighed deeply and looked over at Marley, sitting with Martin. She nodded silently. We turned and headed up the hill.

We scaled the next hill. Dad took water and soaked his handkerchief. I did the same to my bandana and tied it back around my head. Ivy took readings on the GPS unit built into the wafer-thin strap on her pack and sipped water through a tube from a fish-shaped bag attached to her pack. "The C.A.R.P. 5000. Closed Aqua Rehydration Pack is activated," a faint voice crackled from one of the gadgets on her pack.

147

"Copy that," she answered, speaking into the shoulder strap. The computer voice crackled again, the tiny red light blinked in approval. "Roger." Ivy glanced at me sideways. "Systems check."

"Stupid technology," I muttered and turned, nearly running smack into a lichen-covered boulder.

"Hey wait, Dad! There's paint on this rock!" I cried. "It's still wet." I poked my finger into it and gave it a whiff.

"Misty!" Dad called. Across the hill came a faint reply. He called again. The reply got louder. Through the trees came a bouncing, bounding Misty Hills in her flowing skirt and shawl, looking oddly like a woman in a deodorant commercial.

"You'll never believe it, Wolff!" Mrs. Hills called. "I found my painting! You have to see it!" She waved her arms at us.

"Wow, these artists will do anything for their art," Ivy said, chomping her rehydration gum. She pumped up the compressor on her hiking boots to reload. A small fan whirred as her foot air-conditioning system kicked in.

Dad collapsed against a pine, panting. Misty was more than alive, she was glowing. She seemed to float down the hillside carrying her bag of supplies and newly-found painting.

"Be careful, Misty! Slow down!" Dad yelled. "I'm so glad we found you-u-u-oh! Whoa!" Dad tripped backwards over the rock, and in a tangle of limbs and snapping branches—at least I hoped it was branches—tumbled all the way down the hill.

"Holy creeps, Dad! Are you alright?" He gave a little moan

from the bottom of the hill.

"I'm alright, Sugarlumpkins," he called weakly. Misty gasped and ran down the hill.

"Wolff—*Wolff*!" she cried, hopping down the hillside to my dad.

"W-where— *where*?!" screeched Ivy in a panic. She danced around looking left and right. Her oversized pack beeped and blinked a systems overload warning as she lost her balance and went bouncing down the same route as my dad. I couldn't believe it. What were the odds?

WHEN TREES SPEAK—LISTEN!

Ivy rolled and bounced like a shrieking, crunching tumbleweed all the way to the bottom. And she kept screaming once she got there.

"Too bad your anti-falling device didn't activate," I called and smirked. For once it wasn't me doing the falling. I climbed down carefully.

"Arggh!" she yelled "My leg! Don't let the wolf get me." Her eyes rolled in her hemlock-needle-and-duff-encrusted head. "Where's the wolf?" she panted.

"Oh, Ivy dear, I'm sorry," soothed Mrs. Hills. "I meant Wolff, Holly's dad. Not wolf, the furry animal. What are you all doing here anyway?" she turned to Dad.

"We were looking for you, Misty!" he moaned. "We thought you were lost."

"Hello, people," squealed Ivy. "I'm the hurt one here. Ow-w-w-w-ow!" Ivy howled.

"Maybe you shouldn't howl so, Ava," Dad said, looking around. "Your howls of pain could bring in a rival pack."

"I wasn't lost Wolff. I was following my muse," Mrs. Hills smiled. "She, my muse, brought me here to this grove. You'll have to see it. It's magnificent."

Dad grunted and winced. He looked a bit dazed.

"Where are we anyway?" asked Misty. I guess when your

muse calls, you lose all track of time and place.

"I don't really know, Ivy here has the GPS," Dad turned to Ivy, still splayed out on her back.

"Well Mr. Clutzbucket, I'm going out on a busted limb here and say that WE are lost. Because my GPS is kaput after you blazed that downward-facing trail for us." Ivy said, and she howled again.

Dad peeled himself up from the ferns and stood. I handed him his glasses, which I had found on the way down. "What do you mean kaput?" Dad's eyes got big. I measured the sky with my hand.

"What are you doing?" Ivy snarled.

"Seeing how much daylight we have," I answered. "About three hours."

"Oh good! That should get us back well before dark—I could use some coffee," said Mrs. Hills. Wow. I wanted to live in the happy place she lived in. She and Dad tried to lift Ivy.

"Yargh!!" she snarled "Stop! No! it hurts!" They set her down again. Dad adjusted his glasses and scritched his chin, in thinking mode.

"Let me see," Mrs. Hills said, trying to look at Ivy's scraped up leg.

"Like I should trust you, Miss Fairy Wanderbritches?" Ivy cracked, then relented. "Fine. There's a first aid kit in my pack."

Dad unsealed the vacuum lock on her pack and a deflated air

mattress and blanket popped out. Misty dug around and found the first aid kit.

"Irma, I'm going to have to take the pack off your back," Dad said. "It'll be easier to move you. We'll have you fixed up good as new in no time."

"Fine, but I've got my eye on you, big guy," Ivy scowled. Misty inflated the mattress and placed it on the blanket on the ground. Next they helped Ivy scooch onto the mattress. Then Dad used white first aid tape and wrapped the whole thing with Ivy inside like a cocoon. Just her head poked out.

"She looks like a maggot," I said, helping strap Ivy's pack onto Dad's back. Ivy glared at me. "Maybe you should tape her mouth too in case she howls and calls in the wolves," I added as I slung Mrs. Hills' bag over my shoulder and carried her wrapped painting.

"There, you go Irma," Dad said, standing up. "It'll be like riding in a hammock." Misty poked aspirin into Ivy's mouth then gave her a swig of water from her bottle.

"Good going, big lug, but where is it that we are heading?" Ivy's face peeked out the end like an angry red zit ready to burst.

"Good question," said Dad. "Well, we came down the hill so we go back up, right?"

"Sounds like a plan padre," Mrs. Hills said to Dad and they lifted the stretcher. It sagged like a rock in a rug.

"Holy cats in pajamas, why artists? Why couldn't you two be engineers or sailors?" Ivy whined. "Ow-ow-ow! Take it easy!"

"Be brave, Ida! It's pretty steep," said Dad.

"Oh great. I have my life in the hands of Hansel and Gretel and they didn't bring breadcrumbs."

Dad looked around and mumbled. "So many trees," he said, then he suddenly laid Ivy down. He sat in the duff breathing fast. It was like a Martin moment.

"Slow your breathing, Dad," he looked up at me. Mrs. Hills and Ivy looked at each other.

"Let's see. Whew! OK, I'm good. Let's go, team," he said, standing, but fell back down, sweat pouring off his face.

"The forest keeps spinning around us," he said, and fell backwards. Then we heard the sharp crack of two rocks clacking, like a signal.

"Oh, good," said Dad. "Marley must be calling us." Dad tried his whistle, but when he had tumbled down the hill the stupid thing broke.

"OK, get my pack," Ivy sighed. "That button on the strap," she told Mrs. Hills, and pointed with her poky nose at the pack on Dad's back. "There's a built-in airhorn...oh wait, the system is down for upgrades." A blue light slowly flashed on the top of the pack.

"What, no flares?" Dad said impatiently.

"Wolff!" Mrs. Hills snapped, slapping her hand over his mouth. "Listen!" CRASH! Somewhere near us a tree came down—close.

"If a tree falls in the forest and we hear it does that mean it fell on its own or something helped it fall, like a bear?" asked Ivy, her eyes as big as headlamps.

A loud grunt grumbled behind us. A dark form lumbered through the brush up on the hill. Then a great shadow appeared, the sun at its back. My freckles stood on end.

"Trees," squeaked Dad, "So many tree-e-es." He tried to keep from hyperventilating by breathing into the bag from Ivy's emergency blanket. Mrs. Hills sat holding Dad's hand. He looked like he was ready to check out any moment.

"We gotta get outta here pronto like," whimpered Ivy. Then came a loud swish of a tree being shook followed by a grunt. Ivy passed out.

"Yoooo-oop." The shadowy being on the hill stood and waved its arms. "Yoo-hoooooop," it howled again.

"My muse!" Misty said, fumbling for her camera in her bag and snapped a photo of it. "Rats, too dark. Shooting into the sun."

"What?" I asked, "Your muse is Bigfoot? You followed Bigfoot out to its lair?"

"I was singing one morning when it showed up. Then it kept showing up at the cabin. I watched it from the porch," Mrs. Hills shrugged. "It's such a beautiful creature." She sponged Ivy's forehead.

Then the beast on the hill pounded a tree.

"I think it wants to communicate with us, Dad." I whispered. "Dad?" But he sat in a stupor. I decided then and there it was time for action.

"Dad, I'm going up," I said. "I speak Yooper."

"It's not safe, darling," Dad laughed. "Daddy needs a quarter. Anyone got a quarter? I need a candy bar. I'd feel better if I had a candy bar."

"It's waving at us," I said. I tightened my bandana and headed up the hill.

"You can't go," Dad reached out, catching my cargo shorts.

"Dad," I said, "have you ever wrassled an alligator?"

"It was a caiman," he said.

"Ever danced with bears?"

"They were cubs."

"Been with Martin for three days?"

"No, can't say that I have," he said.

"Then I'm going in. Bigfoot left me trail signs, took my walking stick, and then gave it back. That all means something. I've got to meet the native and establish communication."

Dad wheezed. Ivy was out cold again, all the while the roaring groan of frustration went on up the hill until I began walking up through the brush. The sun cast shadows as it dipped below the tree line.

I was about to meet the Wild Yooper.

WILD COMMUNICATION ESTABLISHED

Once I reached the top I was yet again lifted from behind like a mewling kitten. I was carried forty or fifty feet into the trees before I yelled "HEY! Enough already!"

The hairy beast plopped me down on what looked like a low, rough log bench. Or was it a table? Maybe I was dinner!

"I-I come in peace," I said, squinting up at the beast through the speckled sunlight as it towered over me. It grunted then shuffled over to sit on the ground before me with the setting sun at its back. It reached over and pulled out a stick and chewed on it, calmly picking its teeth. It tilted its head this way and that, studying me. Was it wondering if I should be roasted or broiled?

I recognized the big beaver-chew walking stick leaning against a nearby tree. Next to that was a bed of leaves and boughs piled high. Then I noticed lots of stuff laying around. It mostly looked like garbage and stuff left behind by tourists and campers. It moved an empty laundry detergent bottle aside with its foot. The place was very untidy—it must not have been expecting company.

Then bending close it pointed its chewing stick at me. I shut my eyes. Was I about to be a troll shish kabob? It cleared its throat. I opened one eye. That's when I saw a button tucked into its fur. It seemed oddly familiar—where had I seen that before?

The evening sun shone gold on a wrinkled face as ancient as tree-bark beneath a mound of fur. Was I supposed to look it in the eye or not? I suddenly forgot Gram's rules of locking eyes with animals.

"I-come-in-peace," I said again slowly. "I-am-Holly-Wild," I gestured to myself. "I-come-to-make-friends-and-study-your-land-and ways." It gurgled a chuckling cough, then reached over and handed me water from a bark cup. The large rough hands motioned me to drink.

"You," I pointed, "Yooper?" It nodded its head slowly. Then it cleared its throat again.

"Yoo," it imitated in a deep scratchy voice, "yooper?" It talked! I couldn't believe it.

"Me, no—I'm not a Yooper, I am—Hah-lly, Holly." I pointed at my chest. "Me, Holly—you Yooper." I pointed toward it. It leaned back quickly, scared by my sudden move. I put my hand down and smiled with my eyes and freckles instead.

"Me Holly," I repeated to reestablish communication. The beast suddenly sat up, slapped its thigh and exploded in what sounded like laughter.

"Me-hah-lly," it chortled.

"What's so funny?" My freckles sizzled. Here I was, being laughed at by Bigfoot!

"Me Yooper," it chuckled then became quiet.

"You live here?" I gestured around at Bigfoot's home. "I live here—" I held up my right hand, palm out to look like the shape of Michigan, and pointed to where I lived. It seemed so long ago I nearly forgot where Hayfields was.

This started the whole laughing thing all over.

"No Yooper," it shook, its head pointing at me. "Yoo-no-yooooper. Hah-lly." I smiled and nodded. Just like that I had gained the trust of a native Yooper. But was this Yooper a

Bigfoot—or a human?!

The Bigfoot beast and I studied each other in the dappled evening light. I couldn't tell if it was male or female, but it seemed old. From what I could make out, it wore a large dark furred vest with the strange button over a long gray tunic with raggedy-patched leggings. And it was barefoot. Big bare feet! One was bigger than the other and a bit twisted, which must be why it limped through the trees. I was sure this was the same creature Martin and I had encountered.

"Why did you bring me here?" I asked.

"Help. You." It waved toward where we came from.

"Oh," I shivered at the thought of going back to Ivy. And to camp. "I don't need help…"

It grunted and waved. Then I got up the nerve to look it in the eyes. Long, gray scraggly hair fell over its face and stuck out in all directions. A wrinkled brow and clouded pale eyes met mine with a slight scowl. Then the sunburned, soot spattered face broke out into a toothless grin.

A gentle purring sound came from its silvery fur hat. Then the hat yawned and blinked at me. There, perched upon its head and shoulders, was a clattering porcupine!

"Hmm!" the creature hummed, seeming to notice the dying light, then it slapped its thighs and stood up. The porcupine scrambled down and climbed onto the table near me and munched on some bark.

Its massive hands reached under its tunic and pulled out a bark-wrapped package. It ran its finger over it gently then held it very close to its face. Quickly it shuffled around behind me and grabbed an old glass soda bottle filled with liquid. It grunted and thrust it at me.

"No thanks, I'm not thirsty." The cloudy water in the bottle looked worse than the stuff out of a pond. It grunted, shaking

its head no.

"Wolf Girl leg pain," it demonstrated rubbing a leg. Oh, it was for Ivy! It pulled out a rag and motioned. "Soak. Wrap."

"Thank you," I said. I suddenly felt that the creature was a female—and human.

I was feeling less threatened so I looked around camp. A few of the trees had faces like they were carved, like they were watching me. When I looked closer and saw knife marks I realized they were carved!

"Did you do these?" I touched one gently. She grunted and nodded, pushing me.

"So what are you doing out here? Are you homeless?"

"Heh, heh, all home—home everywhere." She spread her arms wide. "Food, water, shelter, fresh air," she motioned about her.

"I want to live in the wilderness like this—like my relatives did." My eyes went back to the weird button like a magnet. She looked down at it, covered it with her hand, then squinted at me.

"It looks familiar. I've seen it before." I explained. I don't know if she heard me as she was pushing me firmly through the brush that surround her camp. She made it clear my visit was over. There was hardly any light left in the woods. The sun was setting and black night comes early to the thick forest.

"One day," she mumbled then shoved the bark package into my backpack and squeezed my shoulder and sent me off. Something about her reminded me of Gram. Gruff, solid, and sturdy—Wild.

"What?" I could barely see anything but tree forms in the dying light. I had so many questions but I started down the slope. When I turned back around—the camp had disappeared into the darkness.

"Wait! Who are you? What's your name? I want to thank you," I called.

"Ha ha, Yooper," came a soft chuckle.

"You left the message on the trail didn't you, the sticks? You painted on the rock!" But there was only silence.

"Thank you—Yooper," I said.

Then I heard Dad and Misty call from below. I was about halfway down when I heard the Yooper call to me.

"Yoo—Ha-lley, Me—Junie." The words were so faint it could have been the wind in the trees. But I heard it all the same. The beast was an old woman named Junie! My head whipped around as I hit the bottom of the slope. The shadows drew over the hill like a heavy curtain. Then it dawned on me—the button! I knew where I'd seen it before! It was all coming together.

Holy creeps times ten. My heart pounded, I was sweating, my freckles burst like freshly popped corn kernels on my face.

I had just looked into the pale eyes of The Wild Yooper, the Bigfoot, Muse and Keeper of the Forest, a true Friend of the Porkies. Beneath the matted hair was not soot but a wild storm of freckles like mine. My missing Wild link and long lost kin—my wild cousin, Pauline Bunyan a.k.a. Pauline Bigge "Junior" a.k.a. PBJ—a.k.a.—Junie!

END OF THE TRAIL

"Dad!" I hollered.

"Holly!" he shouted back. I could barely breathe.

"Dad," I wheezed, trotting to him in the dim glow of Ivy's dying pack.

"Are you OK, Sugarcone?" He was shaking as he squeezed me tight. He looked me over. "Did it hurt you? We gotta get outta here. Now!" He switched on Ivy's hat helmet headlamp. The beam burned through the woods like the light of the Beaver Island Lighthouse.

"Slow down, Dad, I'm fine," I said. "This is medicine for Ivy." I thrust the bottle of liquid and the rag at Mrs. Hills. "From Ju—from your muse." I didn't want anyone to know just yet.

"What in the world is this?" Mrs. Hills asked, holding the bottle up to the light beam.

"Cool it, Shortstuff," said Ivy, who had apparently come to while I was gone. "I'm not drinking pond water from some old beer bottle."

Mrs. Hills opened it and sniffed.

"Oh my! Wow. Strong stuff. It's apple cider vinegar! Helps with pain and swelling." Misty wrapped the soaked bandage around Ivy's swollen black ankle. Ivy couldn't protest much with her arms taped down.

"Hey, that actually feels better. Mush huskies!" Ivy ordered.

"Get me the heck outta here."

We went up and over hills and through the woods. As we made our way over the last hill, we heard calls and could see bobbing lights.

It was Woody and Hunter with Aunt Kitty. They had just crossed the creek and burst through the brush.

"Saw ya a good mile away wit dat light ya got, donchaknow," hollered Woody at Dad. Hunter bayed and leaped. "Ya kits had me worried sick."

"Misty!" Aunt Kitty exclaimed. "You've been found! And what on Earth have you got there? It looks like a giant maggot."

"No, that's Ivy," I chuckled as I took Hunter from Woody so he could help Dad with the stretcher. "Her systems failed and she fell down a hill."

Aunt Kitty pulled out a bag of kale chips, lavender cookies and strong coffee in a thermos for Mrs. Hills, who handed over the bottle of medicine for Ivy's leg. Aunt Kitty opened the cap.

"Whew, apple cider vinegar—with the 'mother'—for healing swollen joints. Good thinking Misty." Mrs. Hills shrugged and looked at me. I shrugged back.

"The Yooper," said Dad. "We saw it. Bigfoot. It gave the stuff to Holly."

"Bigfoot?" yelped Ivy, twisting around to look at us. "You saw Bigfoot? It's really out here? I gotta get back and tell Verna!"

We stood scowling down at Ivy, then Mrs. Hills pulled her camera out of her bag and took a picture of her wrapped in her white cocoon.

"I'm sure the Yearbook Club would love a photo of you showing what you did on your summer vacation," Mrs. Hills said sweetly, "especially with you being the head cheerleader." Ivy's eyes darted from face to face as we stood over her with our arms crossed.

"Um, yeah. Well, I passed out," Ivy stammered. "I didn't never see nothin'."

"Are you sure about that?" asked Dad. Ivy looked at us again, her eyes settling on Mrs. Hills.

"Absolutely," Ivy whispered.

"Good!" said Mrs. Hills. "Let's head back, shall we?"

After Dad tripped three more times, we made it back to the RV. T and Sie were outside with Martin and Marley. Misty squeezed her girls as they rushed to her in excitement. Woody wiped a tear from his eye and honked his schnoz. Everyone decided to spend the last night at Camp Firewood.

When we arrived at Camp Firewood Aunt Kitty and Marley whipped up a regular lumberjack pancake dinner. Woody, Dad and I got a fire going outside. Ivy sat with her vinegar–soaked, ice wrapped bandaged foot propped up on a log, tossing sticks into the fire as Martin played his video game. We all ate syrup-soaked cakes on tin plates under the northern lights that came out and danced all pink and green across the sky.

"You did good today, teams," Marley said to us all. "Or I should say, Team Firewood."

"So Bigfoot is really out there?" asked T, licking the butter off her plastic spork.

"Well," Misty said, "I saw my Muse…."

"And I was given a bottle of healing liquid by the Keeper of the Forest," I said.

"I was rescued by the big, smelly Yooper," Martin added.

Ivy tossed another stick on the fire, then noticed all of us looking at her. "I saw nothin'," she said, looking away.

"Didn't you get a picture of it?" Dad asked Misty.

"Oh, my goodness, I forgot about that!" Misty said, pulling out her camera. "Oh, the light was bad, I was shooting into the

sun. Darn, can't see anything."
The twins groaned. Maybe
I would let them continue
believing that the forest had
secrets. Unexplainable secrets,
magic and awesome mystery,
times ten.

"My momma, I'm sure she's
watching dis right now," Woody
said, looking up. He didn't know
how right he was. Or did he?

Bats and moths floated overhead. Coyotes and owls sang at
the sky show. Woody pulled out a harmonica and we all danced
like wild Yoopers under the U.P stars.

Everyone except Ivy, of course.

My Woodland Muse.

Chapter 26

DAY 7 (SATURDAY)

IT TAKES A WILDERNESS

The next morning before anyone woke, I pulled out the bark wrapped package from my backpack. I untied the leather string and carefully peeled back the birchbark. It was the journal! Pauline had given it back to me! She must have taken it out of my pack the night she carried Martin and me to the trail. I couldn't breathe. I felt like my chest would burst. I was excited but felt strange too. It really didn't belong to me. It should go to Woody. Then I retied the whole thing and slid it deep into my new-old pack.

And just in time, because right then the Vetch family film crew's Death Star pulled up outside. They were there to collect the rest of the "trolls" to return them to their home below the bridge. Verna got out to hunt down Ivy and pick up Vi's luggage. Laser hopped out and stretched. Howler kept the motor running.

I was packing up things for our own trip home and looked around one last time. Woody would have fun running a camp here. I just hoped other kids would have as much fun as we did. Marley was inside cleaning up the cabin and office and packing up her gear. My stomach hurt. I had to find Cousin Woody to give him the journal. He was helping Dad and the twins load gear into the Beast.

"I have a confession to make, Mr. Timberlake," Marley pushed up her glasses. "I was driving back to Camp Firewood after you hired me when I saw Bigfoot cross the road and head into the woods. I had seen an ad earlier for Buzz B Films, promising big bucks for information leading them to Bigfoot. I answered Mr. Vetch's ad. I had student loan bills and I needed the money. When I told them I had the real deal and knew where it hung out they offered double." I looked at Woody.

"The idea to film the kids at camp was a lie," she continued, "to allow them to look for clues. But when I saw how rotten they were, stomping around all over the wildflowers and being mean to the kids, I didn't want to help them anymore. I'm sorry Woody. I really like your camp, and I learned more from the kids than what I taught them. I'll be going to Marquette to look for a job next week."

"No need, little lady," Cousin Woody said, throwing his enormous arm around her tiny shoulders. "You earned yer keep by keeping dose kits safe. We'll get Camp Firewood up ta snuff and you can stay on. If you want." Marley beamed up at him and pulled her hair out of her eyes.

"I was thinking, Woody," said Aunt Kitty as she walked up with Hunter, "maybe you should change the name of the camp

CAMP WILDWOOD

to Camp Wildwood. Firewood may be too confusing for folks."

"I did keep getting people stopping by trying to buy firewood for their camps at the Porkies," Marley smiled shyly.

"Camp Wildwood, hmm, I like dat! I always liked painting. I'll paint a new sign next week."

"What about our camp report cards?" I asked Marley.

"Well," Marley said, looking at her neon green tennis-shoed feet, "I didn't really do a good job as a naturalist, so I tore them up. I think I bored you guys to tears."

"What do you mean?" Martin asked. "You got me in the woods chasing bats. I even stopped being so afraid of stuff and using my inhaler so often."

"You got me to eat veggies and fruits I never did before," I said, "I stopped eating like a possum for a while. But I still like PBJ." Marley smiled weakly.

"We all learned cool survival things," T said. "But more fun, less clipboard." Marley nodded, sighed, then smiled.

"Well, then I officially call it a tie to end your Wilderness Survival Week," she said. "You all did your best."

"What a rip off," Ivy glared, limping past with her suitcase. "Clearly Team S.P.O.R.K. was winner."

"I don't know, Ivy," said Sie, "Holly

showed team spirit and helped her teammate when he was down and out."

"And she persisted putting up with you and Vi," said Martin. "That takes perseverance and prolonged courage." The twins snickered. I had almost forgotten about Vi. She sat in the Death Star staring out the window.

"Persist, prolong, persevere. Good stuff to know," said Sie.

"Whatever, losers, smell ya later," Ivy said, climbing into the Death Star. "I know I'm a winner." She belched loudly.

Martin shook my hand before he got into the giant black RV. "Don't forget," he blinked and tossed his dreads. "Porcupine meatballs, my place."

"Youbetcha," I high-fived him. "You're a real GeEK Martin. You're a good man to ride the river with. Or at least walk along the side of it with." Laser loaded the last bag and the Death Star rumbled out in a cloud of dust and diesel.

"See ya in school Smudgeface," Ivy yelled out the window. I shuddered. School. An icy chill rippled over my back like the frigid waters of Gitchee Gumee. Then I felt a hand give my shoulder a squeeze.

"Young lady," Dad said sternly to me. I wasn't out of the Porky woods yet. "There's a matter of ice and money spending before we got here that needs yet to be dealt with." Oops. I forgot about that. He tried to look bossy and scratched his chin and squinted his freckles at me. It didn't work. My freckles fought back all puppy-like.

"Oh, you're paid up," he grinned. "You did some brave stuff

and I found my comic characters while I was here." He showed us his sketches of Marley, Bigfoot and Woody, The Wildwood Super Yooper Heroes.

"So is that finally the last of the Buckthorns?" asked Sie.

"For now," I said, sighing. Maybe we'd get lucky and her mom would home school her or she'd be sent back a grade—or maybe to military school.

"That's the last of Team S.P.O.R.K. anyway," said T. Mrs. Hills came to get the girls to carry gear. Woody turned around to look at the empty camp. It looked funny and quiet. Empty. My stomach churned. I pulled out the journal from my pack.

SUPER YOOPER "SUPER FOOT"

"I-I found this, here," I said, untying the journal and handing it to Woody. The big guy teared up and touched it gently.

"I already read it," he sniffed. "About a month ago, eh, I found it along da creek close to da artist cabin. I guessed den dat she was still alive. Keepin' an eye on me, donchaknow. I found it, but she gave it to you. That means she wants you to have it." He winked at me. My throat got all tight. I fingered the button on the front of the journal. The very same style of button that hung on Pauline Junior's fur vest. I tucked the journal carefully back into my pack.

"She's nice," I said. I couldn't think of anything else to say. He nodded his head, his red-gray beard bobbing. He wiped a tear away with his giant paw.

"Are you gonna go find her, Woody?" I asked.

"I want to. I remember now when I was a kit, I dreamed of

a hand touching my forehead. Light touch—like a bird's wing. When I woke, it was gone. I like ta think she's been keepin' an eye on me all dese years."

"Maybe she'll visit," I said, blinking back tears.

"Naw, she's feral. She's da voice of da woods, donchaknow," he smiled. "She leaves her mark here and dere. Carving trees, watching over da critters. Picking up garbage," he winked. "She's happy, I reckon." He chuckled.

"So she still uses da vinegar fer her arthritis? Always has," he said. "I remember her limpin' around when I was a kit. Drank da stinkin' vinegar back den, ya. Hated dat smell. Dats how I knowed it was her fer sure."

"She must be making it from the apple trees growing wild out at Nonesuch," I said.

"Yep, it's good ta know she's out dere. Da U.P. wilderness needs a friend."

Aunt Kitty came out to walk Hunter before he was loaded into the Beast. "So I suppose the Bigfoot Emergency Action Search Team is no longer needed," she said. "Why search for Bigfoot when we know it's out there, harmless and helpful. Right Holly?" Aunt Kitty winked at me. I wondered if she knew all along about Pauline, too.

"All aboard!" Dad said, stumbling back out the RV steps. I imagined myself living in the wilderness, swinging through the trees like Tarzan with Kenny, my pet snake, leaping from pine tree to pine tree and not going to school. Living like Pauline Bigge Junior "Bunyan".

"So are we still a team?" Sie pushed me from behind. T grinned, handing me my hat.

"Sure," I said. I took off my headband and hung it from the belt loop of my shorts and put my hat on.

"Thank you," T said. "You look funny without it." They

snickered. Woody gave bear hugs and Marley shook our hands. I climbed the clanky metal steps into the pink-striped Beast. The engine roared, but Dad was outside with Mrs. Hills and the twins. I looked in the cab and nearly fell backwards over the kitchen table.

"Gram!"

"How was the forest, Holly?" she turned around. I hopped over a bag of groceries and gave Gram a hug around the neck.

"Miss me, Sugar Pie?" she said.

"Yeah, I did. A little bit," I blinked. "But isn't Dad coming?" I peeked out the window for him. We had spent so little time together on this trip!

"No worries, he's flying copilot," Gram whispered. "I'm captain now. I've seen him drive this rig." He climbed in and shut the door.

"Dad, don't you have to get back home?" I asked him.

"Misty inspired me. I'm going to look for my muse and try some new things. Breathe new life into my work," he said. "I hope to find inspiration out east. After getting the van taken care of, your Gram brought Aunt Kitty's car here so she can take off to do some study—below the bridge."

I hadn't even noticed her tiny sticker-covered wagon with its bike and kayak when the Death Star left. I must have been really relieved to see Ivy go to miss that clue! Aunt Kitty came inside to say goodbye. I'd miss her and Hunter.

"So where are we headed?" I asked, looking for my Team.

"This rig is heading to Picture Rocks National Lakeshore

and Hiawatha National Forest. You saw the west and now we go east," said Gram, checking mirrors and adjusting duct tape.

"Take notes and drop me a line," Aunt Kitty said with a hug. "Our trails will cross again, soon." Then she winked at me and giggled. "You really do look like her!" she said and climbed into her car. This time I knew who she was talking about.

Mrs. Hills and Sie and T climbed the steps inside.

"Where's your gear? Packed in back?" I asked, ready for my team to continue our journey eastward. We had not done Team stuff in a while. We had a lot more to explore.

"Mom wants us to stay with her," said Sie. The twins hung their heads and wouldn't look at me.

"B-but—but our expedition! The Yoopers!" I stammered. "We were going to explore and establish GeEK contact up here—together."

"I know," said T, fidgeting.

"I'm finished here next week," Mrs. Hills said, looking pained. "They were at their Dad's this summer, then off adventuring with you, and then I was up here. I've missed my girls. They've really grown." she misted up. I understood. It hurt, but I understood.

"See you when you get home," said T, yanking on her pine cone hair bob.

"If I make it home," I said, pouting and blinking back tears.

"You'll come home, freak," Sie said, punching my shoulder. "You're the mighty Holly H. Wild. Besides, we have to find out who our teachers are." I nodded my head.

"We can swap adventure stories when we see you," said T. My stomach hurt. Fifth grade, new teachers, Ivy. The thought haunted me. I nodded again. This summer was whizzing by far too fast.

"There's more to explore," I mumbled, pulling my hat down over my eyes.

"Team Wild!" shouted Sie and T, striking their super silly super hero pose. It made me laugh and we all gave high fives and hugs. Mrs. Hills gave me an extra big hug.

"From your mom," she said. I couldn't watch as they climbed down the steps and latched the door.

How could I explore the Pictured Rocks and Hiawatha National Forest without my Team? I had just gotten my Team back and then they were gone just that quick. The Beast gave a mighty Ivy belch as we lurched out of the Porcupine Mountains Wilderness Area.

I sat at the table and pulled the journal out of my pack. I

rubbed the star button on the front cover. My stomach felt funny. We had done so much cool stuff. Now it was just Dad and Gram and me. I dropped my head on the table. Being a lone wolf wild and free and swinging from trees didn't seem so neat right now. One thing I learned in the wilderness forest and a survival rule that Marley missed was companionship. Like the forest community we all need each other to survive. I needed my Team.

Just then there was honking and the flashing of lights. It was Aunt Kitty's car with the wildly swinging red kayak and bike. Hunter's ears and tongue flapped in the breeze. Gram swung the RV over to the side of the road. Aunt Kitty rushed to Gram's door.

There was a banging outside the RV. I opened the cabin door and there stood Woody with T and Sie!

"You fergot some kits Wolff!" he bellowed over the Beast's throaty engine. The twins climbed aboard as Woody shoved their mother ship bag inside.

"W-what?" I stammered. "How?"

"I don't know," Sie said. "It was weird. Suddenly Mom remembered she couldn't keep kids at the artist cabin and Aunt Kitty said she could catch you."

"Those artist types," I said, pushing their gear in the back.

"So here we are!" T burst. "We get to go too!"

"Awesome times ten!" I yelped. "Team Wild back together again! And boy, do I have a lot to tell you guys!"

"Gram," I yelled, "I'll be needing a new pair of boots when we get to a town," I grinned, looking at my feet. I was hanging up this pair of moccasins to pass down to my granddaughter one day.

Wilderness—forever protected and free. An eagle flew over Lake Superior as we headed east into the morning sun. We'd join the caravan of migrating RVs as they headed back to the bridge that linked the north and south—the upper and lower peninsulas of Michigan.

I pulled out my journal for my last Porkies entry.

One day, Pauline had told me. One day I would be ready to survive on my own. My Wild family tree had survived storms, pruning, fire and flood like the forest of the Porkies and like so many families do. We are all survivors. We all have a job, a skill, a purpose. Someone to keep us organized, someone to make us laugh, and someone to give bear hugs. No one gets voted out in families. No one. As the Beast roars onto the highway, I look down at my feet—one shorter than the other, and wiggle my toes. Wanderlust Gram had called it the day she had given me my new, old backpack. One day, Pauline had said. One day.

The rest of our party will continue our Wild Yooper exploration of this strange new land, this wild Upper Peninsula of Michigan. It's good to know that the team is there when the waters get rough and the trail narrows.

Surviving the wilderness requires teamwork.

ABOUT THE AUTHOR

*Artist, author/illustrator, Lori Taylor was
artist-in-residence for the Porcupine Mountains Wilderness
State Park in 2008, where she wandered the wild for two weeks
but did not see Bigfoot—yet later heard tales of it there.*

*Like the lumberjack storytellers of old, Lori born in
Pontiac, MI, (who lived in the town of Holly as a toddler) was
often referred to by her mother as the "Holly Herald"
for the stories she wove as a child.*

*Today Lori lives in Pinckney, MI where she writes
and illustrates the tales of her explorations.*

Trees throughout America are rapidly disappearing right now, leaving wildlife like screech owls, chickadees, flying squirrels and more without cavities to nest in. Help restore and reforest crucial habitat for wildlife in need. Plant a tree or support organizations that plant trees.

Blue jays, turkeys, robins and raccoons rely on trees with fruits and nuts, while hummingbirds and insects need the nectar from the flowers of fruit-bearing trees.

Wood frogs, toads, salamanders and other amphibians use fallen leaves and logs for shelter in the fall.

Otters, turtles, and fish need clear, clear water. Trees planted near streams reduce soil erosion and filter pollutants.

There are 30,000 quills on a porcupine's back, and 32,000 acres of old growth forest in the Porcupine Mountains. Hug a tree. Play in the parks!

Get Going and Get Growing!

For more more info on the
Friends of the Porkies or wilderness, visit:

http://porkies.org/
www.wilderness.org

ENTER

THE

FOREST

CRYPTIC CREATURES

HANDLE HOUND

tail sweeps out tracks and mess!

can swallow axe whole for quick get-away.

5' tall

WHO DUNNIT?

Many cultures told tales of cryptic (secret) creatures to warn, entertain and explain mysterious events in wild places.

The lumberjacks wove wild tales of these creatures to pass the time during the long, cold, dark winter nights.

Most stories were based on actual events and experiences.

Look for clues of each beast in Holly's story!

"AXE HANDLE HOUND"

A creature who raids camps at night and nibbles the handles off axes and shovels.

What nocturnal forest animal could have done this? Why?

"HIDE-BEHIND"

This sneaky beastie hides behind trees waiting to snatch your mittens or lunch.

What shy forest animal could have done this deed?

hides behind trees and steal's mittens

SHLURRP!

...when one is not looking

HIDE BEHIND

180

AGRO PELTER

tosser
of sticks
and howler
of forest

monkey-faced
timber terror!

"AGROPELTER"

A beast who lives high in the tree's canopy and howls like a monkey and drops sticks on folks.

What forest animal could have done this?

TINGS DAT GO BUMP IN DA **NIGHT!**

Cryptozoology, *crypto* (hidden or covered) and *zoology* (the study of animal life) is a study and search for legendary animals a.k.a. "cryptids".

DRAW your own cryptic creature and tell its tale!

DECIDUOUS LEAF MAGIC!

Deciduous trees DECIDE to lose their leaves! Which means to say that they drop their leaves in fall.

Marley's Leaf Cup

Pick a large green maple leaf from a maple tree. FOLD right side in, then the left. Hold in place as you FOLD the bottom up to make a cup! Holds water or trail Gorp!

Sugar
Maple Leaf

2
1
3

Tierra's LEAFY Survival Fashion!

No sleeping bag--no problem! Make like a squirrel and gather dry leaves and ferns. Stuff them into your clothes and socks to stay warm (the more the better). For extra warmth, make a pile of leaves and climb inside--like a squirrel.

CONIFEROUS LEAF MAGIC!

Coniferous trees are cone-shaped, "evergreens", trees that have needle leaves and cones on their branches. Pines, hemlocks, firs and spruce are coniferous trees. How can you tell the difference between spruce and pine? Shake hands with a tree! If it has stiff, short poky needles that are not in "bundles" it is probably a spruce. White pine needles are soft and are in bundles of 5 needles on the branch.

5 needle leaves in a bundle spell out W-H-I-T-E pine!

White Pine Needles

white pine cone 3-5"

hemlock cone 1/2"

Misty's Refreshing Pine Needle Tea

Cut 1/2" pieces of fresh white pine needles (one large handful).

Place pieces on unbleached coffee filter.

FOLD filter in half, STAPLE closed to make a large TEA BAG.

Carefully DROP bag into water that has been boiled. BE careful!

STEEP tea for 20 minutes to half hour. REMOVE bag. Add COLD water to taste or drink warm!

Pine Tea is a beautiful plum-purple brown color and packs more of a Vitamin C punch than oranges!

LAKE SUPERIOR! FYI!

a.k.a. "Gichigami", "Big Water", by Ojibwe, penned as "Gitche Gumee" by 1800s explorer Henry Schoolcraft and called "superior" by French traders because it was above the other lakes.

🌀 Lake Superior is the LARGEST of Great Lakes in area and volume!

🌀 The largest surface area of any freshwater lake in the WORLD! 31,700 square miles.

🌀 Average depth is 483' and is 1,333' deep just off Grand Island!

184

Big Carp River Trail (Escarpment)

Escarpment, from the Italian word *scarpa* meaning "shoe", is a steep cliff or slope formed by faults or erosion. Escarpments separate two level areas of land.

The water at the top is Lake Superior. Lake of the Clouds is below that and the Big Carp River runs through the foreground.

Color the rock walls red. Color the deciduous trees the colors of summer or autumn. Color the sky and water the same color.

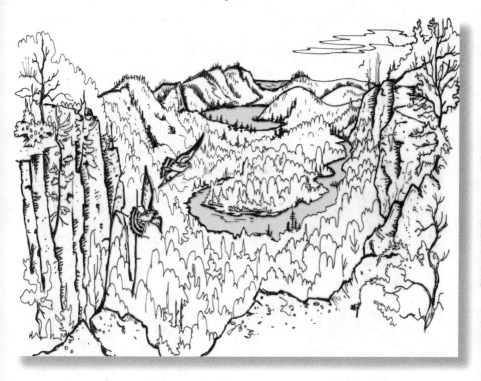

"*Kag-wadjiw*", the Ojibwe people called the chain of mountains rising from the waters of Lake Superior. They reminded them of "kag", the woodland Porcupine.

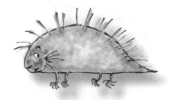

DON'T BE FOOLISH LIKE IVY!

The PORKIES' forest, like most forests, have many flowers that produce pretty, colorful berries.

LOOK only, NEVER pick or eat a BERRY you find on the trail! What looks like a blueberry could make you very sick! Some berries are extremely poisonous!

BE SAFE, THINK FIRST!

STARFLOWER

BLUEBEAD LILY

BUNCHBERRY

WHITE BANEBERRY A.K.A. "DOLL'S EYES"

CHECKERBERRY

BEARBERRY

WILDERNESS SURVIVAL GAME

Two GeEK players take turns drawing one line at a time to make a square. When a square is made on your turn place your initial inside for 1 point. Add extra points by finding a SURVIVAL item! Remember that planning and preparing is part of survival! Persist, prolong and persevere!

shelter: 4 pts.

fire: 3 pts.

water: 3 pts.

food: 2 pts.

Rules of Survival 4! 4 minutes without AIR, 4 hours without SHELTER, 4 days without WATER, 4 weeks without FOOD!

Player 1 _____   Player 2 _____

Eye SHINE Colors

Porcupine - RED
Skunk - AMBER
Flying Squirrel - RED-ORANGE
Deer - SILVER-WHITE
Fox - WHITE
Raccoon - YELLOW
Coyote/Bobcat - GREEN-GOLD
Dog/Cat - GREEN

COLOR in the animal's eye shine color

THE FOREST HAS 1,000 EYES!

PORCUPINE
FACTS & TRACKS

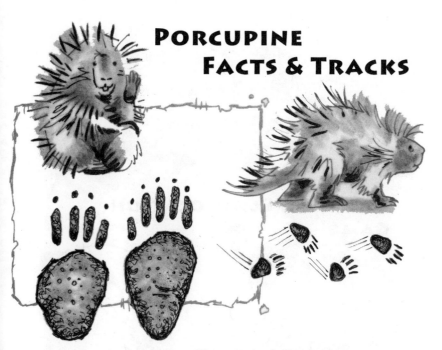

front   rear

QUILL
3" - 5"

There are 30,000 quills on a porcupine, but not on their face or belly. Quills are spongy-filled specialized hairs. The sharp, dark tips have overlapping scales that appear barbed. Once imbedded in skin the scales pull the quill deeper!

Porky Threat Display!

Porkies DO NOT shoot or throw quills! They turn their back and can raise their quills and swipe their tail to deliver a blow.

STUFF TO DO

BAT! BUG! ECHOLOCATION GAME

"BAT!"

"BUG"

Have group stand in a circle. Select a "BAT". Blindfold the bat. Select a "BUG". Now the fun begins. BAT calls out "bat!" and BUG answers the bat by calling "bug!" so the BAT can find its meal (Like the "Marco Polo" game). BUG can move around and hide INSIDE the circle. When BAT finds BUG the game is over.

HOLLY AND MARTIN'S BRUSH SHELTER

Find long, sturdy BRANCHES for support frame and lean them against a tree. Forked ones hold best.

Find fallen BRUSH found on the ground: ferns, leaves, sticks, pine boughs and forked branches as filler.

Leaning or fallen trees make a good base!

HOLLY'S BANDANA USES!

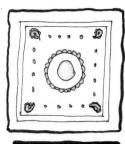

fold

1. HOLD hair in place and look sweet like a French trader.

2. HOLD food or gorp (emergency gathering bowl)

3. HEAD and NECK shade placed under hat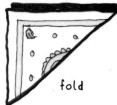

4. COLD compress to avoid overheating. Dip, wring out, tie on.

5. BUG swatter! Like a horse tail, swing while hiking to keep pests off.

6. MOUTH & NOSE cover for campfire smoke, dust, smelly big feet odors, etc.

7. EMERGENCY handkerchief. DO NOT use on head afterward--rinse after use!

8. FLAG to signal or mark camp.

9. BLINDFOLD for playing games like "BAT! BUG!"

10. WHAT else can you think of? Be creative!

Misty Hills' "Touch the Earth Day!"

Walk about in moccasins
or barefoot. Feel the
ground beneath your feet.
Write about it.

"Touch the Earth Art!"

Supplies: Builder's Paper (or large sheets)
Carbon Drawing Sticks
Charcoal Sticks or Crayon

carbon
stick

Roll out a sheet of builder's paper to draw on the
ground. Draw an outline of the horizon or furthest
you can see. Then draw the closer tree outline. Next
draw what is in front of you and on the ground! Don't
forget to add the date and place at the bottom.

ARTIST-IN-RESIDENCE

What is an artist-in-residence? An artist chosen by a state or national park, or other group to go out and spend time for 2-3 weeks carefully observing the land to tell its story with art. In painting, drawing, poetry or song, the artist tells an important tale that preserves what makes that area a special place and to get folks there to enjoy it.

Be an artist-in-residence on your next vacation or in your own backyard. First, what captures your attention in your special spot?

Sit there a while and listen, look and smell and touch.

Now try painting with oil pastel, crayon or chalk on cardboard, heavy paper or canvas sheets. Misty used oil pastels and oil paint straight out of the tube on heavy paper.

For further inspiration, check out the awesome early 20th century work of Canadian artists, the Group of Seven, Tom Thomson and Emily Carr. Both Emily and Tom loved the trees, wild places and parks of Canada.

See how they saw nature and try copying their style of making nature into simple, playful shapes and thrilling colors!

Artists are important for everyone, especially when it comes to telling nature's story. They are our eyes and ears that help us learn to care about the earth! Hug an artist today!

LISTENING TO THE TREES!

*The forest is a family where the
young live and grow in the shade of their elders!*

FOREST ADVICE
- Be flexible like hemlock.
- Stand tall like birch.
- Always share your fruits and nuts.
- Dance in the sun like poplar.
- Stretch your limbs like oak.
- Be sweet like maple.
- Sing like pine.
- Remember your roots.
- Drink plenty of water.
- Go out on a limb.
- BREATHE and hug a tree!